A Very
DRAGON
Christmas

DRAGON GUARD BOOK 51
MACALLEN FAMILY CLAN

by
JULIA MILLS

There are no coincidences
The Universe does not make mistakes
Fate will not be denied.

JOIN THE CLAN!

Wanna Keep Up With All My Crazy? Wanna have fun? Win
some cool prizes? Get *exclusive* excerpts to upcoming books?
Sign up for my newsletter RIGHT HERE!
Be the FIRST to see new covers, sneak peeks, and best of all,
ADVANCED COPIES OF ALL MY BOOKS!!!
Join the group! Julia's Mills' Fan Club on Facebook!
I absolutely LOVE stalkers!
You can find the links to follow me everywhere
at JuliaMillsAuthor.com!

ACKNOWLEDGMENTS

Edited by Em Edits
Proofread by Book Nook Nuts
Beta Read by Linda Levy

For my mom

The Dragon Guard

We soar the skies
Free to a certain extent.
As long as we stay hidden
From prying human eyes.

Our scales differ in color
Our defensive weapons,
Tails, horns, talons and all,
Are never the same.

We are one with nature
We blend in with nature
The wind helps us soar high in the heavens
While the earth grants us healing strength in our hour of need.

We are one with the world
We are the guardians of our kin
When evil conspires to maim and hurt
We are protectors of this human race.

As majestic animals of fairytales
We share our beings with great men
They walk in honor and the grace of Fate.
Fate that we cannot deny.

A VERY DRAGON CHRISTMAS

The Desert holds many secrets, but are there Christmas miracles, too?

This ain't your momma's fairy tale.
When the clock strikes midnight on Christmas Eve, Abbie will lose more than her glass slipper if she hasn't found her Mate.

Abbie's prayin' for a very Dragon Christmas,
all she needs is Cass.

INDEX OF THE ORIGINAL LANGUAGE OF THE DRAGON KIN AND THE THORNTREE CHEROKEE TRIBE

Scottish Gaelic (Spoken by Dragons of the Clan of Maeve from the Isle of Skye)

Rianadair..........Tracker

Mo charaid ghràdhach..........My dear freind

Mo Anam Aharaid.......... My Soul Mate

My love ....Mo ghràdh

My heart ....Mo chridhe

Mo stór.......... My treasure

Deid Cuddie............Dead Horse

Beannaichte Le Lomadh Spiorad ....Blessed with Many Spirits

M'eudail..........My Sweetheart

Tha mo chridhe taobh a-staigh thu a-nis agus gu bràth..........My heart d within you now and forever

Bho a-nis gu deireadh an ama bheir mi gràdh dhut le mo chridhe uile..........From now until the end of time I will love you with all my heart

Cherokee

Skeenah.........Demon

Uktena..........Dragon

BONUS CHRISTMAS CHAPTER

GOLDEN FIRE CLAN

Hey y'all! I published this Bonus Chapter in the Holidays With The Dragons Box Set.
However, A Very Dragon Christmas, Cass and Abbie's Story, the one you are about to read, starts right after this bonus chapter.
Sooooooo...
I figured I had better include it here for all those who did read the box set.
If you already have, no worries!
Just flip to Chapter One and get started with
A Very Dragon Christmas!
I just cannot wait to hear what you think of Cass and Abbie's story!
Merry Christmas! Happy Holidays!
And a VERY HAPPY NEW YEAR!
XOXO, Julia, Liz, Em and all the furbabies

The Holiday Season 2024
Golden Fire Clan

"**P**lease tell me that I have nothing to worry about. That because my boys are still asking for video games, new tablets, and remote-control cars for Christmas, they are *years* from going through their... their... Well, crap, I can't even say the freakin' word."

"Their first Shift?" Kyndel finished Grace's thought with the lilt of a question in her tone.

"Yeah, that. I mean..." Gasping loudly, she hurried on, the regret in her voice scenting the room with a sharp, spicy aroma. "Oh, shit! I am the worst friend ever!" Sniffling, Kyndel could tell that her bestie was just barely holding it all together.

She was also well aware that the highly accomplished lawyer had to say her peace–had to get it all out–before she could offer advice and comfort. So, she held her tongue, kept pitting fruit, and waited less than a single beat of her heart before Grace added, "I'm so sorry. Look at me worrying about myself when you..."

After three whole seconds of silence, what seemed like a lifetime to Kyndel because she wanted so badly to comfort her friend, she slid her eyes to the left. She wasn't surprised to find Grace staring at the cabinet while peeling the same strip off the same apple for what looked like the fourteenth time because the little black seeds were peeking through the flesh. At the rate she was going, there'd be no apple left at all. It was time to rescue the poor fruit–and her friend.

Reaching over, Kyndel gently placed one hand on Grace's, then used the other to pluck the abused apple from her fingers. Placing what was left of Johnny Appleseed's favorite food with the others she'd peeled for pies, she put her arm around Grace's shoulders and steered her to the closest chair. Once she was sure her bestie wouldn't slide onto the floor and end up in a fetal position, paralyzed with worry, she put the side of the index finger of her left hand under the illustrious lawyer's chin. Then she lifted it until they were looking into one another's eyes. The worry she saw in those brilliant blue peepers kicked all her protective instincts into overdrive and had her saying exactly what needed to be said to help her friend feel better.

"Alright, time to stop beating yourself up for things you cannot control. Yes, you are our very own Superwoman, but even she had to deal with that nasty kryptonite. Give yourself a break, my love. Take a deep breath, let it all go, then listen to old Auntie Kyndel."

With a weak smile, Grace did exactly as she instructed. Once she'd taken a deep cleansing breath and let it out, Kyndel went on, "First of all, you have never been nor will you ever be a bad friend. You are the best, and that's all there is to it."

She didn't miss a beat as she winked, gave a sharp nod, and powered on. "Secondly, I know what you're going through, and everything you feel is absolutely normal. Lastly, and most importantly, listen and listen well 'cause you know beyond a shadow of a doubt that you can trust what I'm sayin'."

Stopping again, this time to give her bestie 'the look'. The one where she opened her eyes wide, gave a single, pointed nod, and tilted her head to the side until the person she was looking at smiled. Crinkling her nose in the silliest way possible, waiting until Grace gave her a weak grin, Kyndel went right back to what she had been saying. "Hell, you know almost as well as I do that watching Jay Shift for the first time was the most shocking thing I'd seen in... in..." Shrugging and exhaling sharply, she powered on. "Well, in about eleven years." She added a chuckle with the hopes of continuing to lighten the mood. "Seeing Rayne and the others become full-sized Winged Warriors was nothing compared to watching my son become a Berserker Dragon. I didn't even know he could do that until he was at least a hundred years old. Talk about being kicked in the ass by Aunt Nettie's mule. It was nuckin' futs."

"Yeah," Grace breathed, slowly nodding with her eyes so wide that she resembled a deer caught in headlights.

"Yeah," Kyndel emphatically agreed, hoping to put some life back into the person she'd known the longest in the world. "So, you know that I understand *exactly* what you're going through, and to be honest, I'm glad I experienced it first."

"You are?"

"Hell, yeah, I am," Kyndel adamantly confirmed. "I only have one son. You've got a matched set. At least, you got to see a sneak preview of what's comin' down the pike. At least you've seen the Shift part, no matter what form the twins take. So, it won't be a complete shock. And let's not forget what Carrick, the Elders, and Siobhan said..."

"Oh, yeah, I remember," Grace agreed with silent laughter, her shoulders slightly bouncing up and down. Right after Jay Shifted back to... Well, he Shifted back to my fantastic godson, Jay." Closing her eyes for a second, she shook her head, grinned, and looked back at Kyndel. "Sorry, it's just still so hard to fathom."

"Girl, who you tellin'?"

"For real!" She snickered, then continued. "Now, what was I sayin'? Oh, yeah, Carrick and the whole gang said that when one of my boys Shifts for the first time, the other will follow within minutes." Another sigh, this one with more gusto and a bit of a hiccup of a giggle at the end, and she went on, "Then, after we got home and the boys were asleep, Aidan said that's how it was with him and Aaron."

"And let me guess, Big A..." (The nickname Aaron, the oldest of the O'Brien twins, was given at a young age and was still called hundreds of years later.) "...agreed when you asked him?"

"I didn't even have to ask," Grace shrugged. "He and Charlie came over the next day under the guise of picking up a book I said they could borrow, and Aaron slid it right into the conversation."

"He's good like that," Kyndel laughed.

"You know it. Gotta love my brother-in-law."

"Yeah, we do, even when he puts both feet in his mouth."

"True," Grace nodded. "I did get a good laugh when Charlie swatted his arm. I do so love her."

"Me too," the feisty redhead agreed. "And now, you listen to old Kyndel here, and listen good as I drop some Southern wisdom straight from Granny on ya'. A*lways, always, always* be prepared for anything."

"Girl, you've been telling me that since the day I realized why you were hanging out with that big, hunky hubby of yours and then found out that Dragons are real and men can turn into them."

"See there? I do get it right every once in a while."

"More like all the damn time."

"Shh." She raised her index finger to her lips and gave Grace her best silly grin. "Don't tell those boys of mine. I like to keep Rayne and Jay guessin'. They think they can get stuff over on me, and it's fun when I get to catch 'em at it."

Loving that her friend was finally truly relaxing, Kyndel had one more thing to add. "Like I was sayin', and you know this all too well because you've said it to me more than once, always be prepared for anything, but do *not* let the expectations, or in some cases–the fear and dread–weigh you down. If we've learned anything, it's that shit is gonna happen, and there's nothing we can do to change that fact, but we can duck and weave better than the average Dragon's Mate. The Heavens know that we're experts at gettin' outta the way."

Finally smiling with the confidence Kyndel had come to expect, Grace readily agreed, "I know you're right." Reaching up as her bestie moved her hand, the lawyer tucked a few errant strands of ebony hair that had fallen out of her ponytail behind her ear and sighed as if the weight of the world had suddenly returned to her shoulders. "It's just that..."

"It's just now that you know it can happen early, that you've seen it with your own eyes, you're wondering if Ash and Ang are ready. You know you're not ready, but it's not you who will have to go through it all, and there is nothing on this big blue and green ball we call home that we won't do to keep our boys safe–the big ones and the young ones."

"Yeah, that about sums it up."

"Well, like I told you that day, and pretty much every day since then, you're gonna feel everything they feel, and you're gonna be so glad that you did. Yes, it is special and wonderful to share it with your Mate, but nothing compares to sharing it with your child. I promise you're gonna be just fine. You are Grace mutherhumpin'-Kensington-O'Brien, dammit. You got this and don't need a T-shirt or a bag of chips."

With her smile gaining strength, Grace wrinkled her nose. "How do you always know exactly the right thing to say?"

"Oh, girl, come on now," Kyndle laughed out loud. "You know I have the gift of gab and learned to baffle 'em with bullshit when I can't dazzle 'em with brilliance from the best teacher in the whole world, my Granny."

"Thank God for Granny Masterson."

"You can say that again. Pretty much all I know about gettin' from one minute to the next and puttin' one foot in front of the other when I feel like givin' up, I learned from that woman, and I damn sure have applied it more times than I can remember in the last week. However..." She stopped, propped her hands on her hips, and started back up right where she'd left off. "...what I had to figure out on my own was that those boys of ours are way more ready for their Destiny than we are." Chuckling as she turned to make a fresh pot of coffee because she was sure they both needed it, she added, "Nothin's changed in that department since the day they were born."

"No shit," Grace snorted, letting Kyndel know her dearest friend was doing good. "Just like when all three of them walked before they were six months old, and Siobhan just laughed, telling us that it was only the beginning of raising a child blessed by the Universe."

"Or when we caught the three of them climbing that huge tree that damn near reaches the clouds a month before Jay's fourth birthday, and Zachary laughed and said we were lucky it was a tree and not a mountain."

"Or when they were building a treehouse in that same damn big oak less than a year later."

"Without the help of any of us," Rayne and Aidan laughed as they walked into the kitchen.

"I still can't figure out how they reached the tools in the shed," the Commander chuckled.

"Or how they knew the right nails to get and where to find them in my toolbox," Grace's Mate snorted.

Meeting her hubby halfway, Kyndel pushed up on her toes, let her fingers tangle in the brown, silken curls curling at the collar of his soft, gray T-shirt, and looked into his lavender eyes. Leaning into his wonderfully muscular chest, she kissed the man made for her by the Universe with everything she had.

He was the miracle that continued to amaze her every day. And the fact that her heart did that silly little pitter-pat every time she laid eyes on him was one of the best things she'd ever experienced.

Eleven years had only made what she felt for her Mate stronger–and there was no doubt he returned those feelings in every single way. He truly was her other half. Rayne completed her in ways she hadn't known she needed until she met him on that fateful night. Whatever she'd done right in a past life, she thanked God, the Heavens, and anybody else she could think of every single day for bringing her Dragon into her life.

"I love you, too, Mo ghrá." His whispered affection floated through her mind.

It let her know that their hearts and souls were blessedly connected for the rest of forever. It made her heart skip a beat and goosebumps jump to attention all over her body. The plethora of love and devotion they shared had her deepen their kiss until she forgot where they were and that they most definitely were not alone.

Of course, at that exact moment, the 'peanut gallery'– her nickname for Jay, Ash, and Ang— also decided to enter the kitchen and provide unneeded and unwanted commentary.

"Oh, gross!" Groaning and gagging as only a preteen can do, Jay dragged the last word out as long as he could

Not be outdone, Ashton, aka Ash, the oldest of Grace and Aidan's twins by four minutes, griped, "Could y'all not do that in the kitchen? Any of y'all? You do know it's where we eat, right? Dadgummit, this is my happy place, and y'all are throwin' around cooties like they're confetti."

But it was Angus, also known as Ang, who had them all laughing when he chimed in with, "All this kissy face stuff *almost*, and yes, that is *just almost*, makes me lose my appetite. It's bad enough that Mom and Dad are always making lovey-dovey eyes at each other, but come on, Aunt Kyndel and Uncle Rayne. Y'all are killin' me here. I thought you had my back."

"Dude, just wait till you find the woman the Universe made for you," Rayne teased, his attempt at being a surfer almost as funny as what he was saying. "She's gonna have you all tied up in your fruit of the looms. You're not gonna know what hit you, but you're gonna love every minute of it, and your pops and I are gonna have the time of our lives makin' fun of you."

"Awww, gross, Dad!"

"You boys are killing me," Kyndel hummed, just barely containing her laughter.

Making a show of pulling away from her Mate–complete with what looked like a dip to rival anything Fred Astaire and Ginger Rogers ever did, she let the back of her hand float dramatically onto her forehead. Then, in the best Scarlett O'Hara impersonation she could muster, she poured even more Southern in her accent than was already there and teased, "Come on, boys, this is what real love looks like. Soak it up."

As the kitchen erupted in laughter, she stood up straight and slowly turned, sure to stay close to her hubby. Not only did she love being near him and knew it embarrassed her son in all the best ways, but Rayne's touch caused the best tingles in the whole wide world.

Loving that her Mate kept his hands around her waist, she tried to look stern but knew she'd failed when the laughter from all three boys grew with such wild abandon that there were happy tears rolling down their cheeks. Giving them a wink when they'd almost calmed to their usual, although be it uproarious state, she leaned back into Rayne's ever-waiting embrace. Soaking in the warmth that always came from her hubby, she matter-of-factly stated, "You know what? You boys always seem to forget how you got here." Waggling her eyebrows at Grace, she went on, "Without all this kissy face, none of y'all ever would've been..."

"NO!" Jay shrieked, closing his eyes so tightly that only the tiniest bit of his long, dark lashes were still visible. Slapping his hands over his ears, he sang, "La-la-la-la-la-la," at the top of his lungs before adding, "Make it stop! Make it stop! Please, if you love me at all, make it stop!"

Loving that her son could be such a goofball, Kyndel looked at her godsons and could no longer hold back her laughter. It had to be one of the funniest things she'd seen in a long time. Ash had his hands over his brother's ears, and Ang had his over Ash's, and together they were dancing around singing, "We can't hear you! We can't hear you! Nanny-nanny-boo-boo."

"Once again, it's a tossup," Aidan, Grace's Mate, one of the renowned O'Brien twins, snorted with laughter.

"You mean which one of our boys gets the award for being just as crazy as we were at that age?" Rayne guffawed with such gusto that Kyndel felt the glorious vibrations in her back.

"You know it," Aidan nodded. Still chuckling, his hands on Grace's shoulders, Kyndel watched with sisterly love as he affectionately massaged away what was left of his Mate's worries. "Thank the Heavens we all have each other."

"Hell yeah, it's the only way we're not outnumbered,"

Kyndel chimed in. Then, looking at Grace, she winked. "See? Things are gonna be just fine."

"And if they aren't, we'll just fix 'em, then laugh about it for years to come."

"There ya' go!" Remembering that her hubby had returned way sooner than she'd expected, Kyndel turned back around, looked her Mate in the eye, and asked, "And what brings you home so early, Mr. Man? I thought you were..."

"You thought we were deep in the woods, getting Christmas trees for our house, Aidan and Grace's, and the Great Hall?"

"Yep," she nodded, stepping back as the coffeemaker dinged, letting her know it was ready. "You got it in one. So, what's up?"

"We didn't even get out of the Lair," Rayne sighed. "Lance stopped us before we made it as far as the truck."

At the mention of another of his Brethren, the Golden Dragon of their Clan and Mate to one of Kyndel's dearest friends, Dr. Samantha Malone-Kavanaugh, the curvy redhead spun around so quickly the kitchen was a blur before she stopped to spear her hubby with a worried look. Her hands moved in time with her words, as they always did when she was making a point or excited, and she fired off questions like bullets from an old Tommy gun. "Is everything okay? It's not the baby, is it? Sam's got about five weeks before she's due. Did Lance say it was the baby? Or that Sam's not feelin' well? Maybe I should..."

"You should take a deep breath," Rayne assured. "Get your coffee, sit down, and I'll tell you exactly what's goin' on. No need to freak out just yet."

"Don't forget that our babies can come early with no

issues at all," Grace reminded. "Not even you made it all forty weeks."

"Yeah, yeah, yeah, you're right," Kyndel agreed, feeling a little better. "But you know I worry." Hurrying to fill not only her mug but also Grace's, then grabbing Rayne and Aidan a bottle of water, she asked the boys, who were looking on, "Y'all need somethin' before I sit down?"

"Nope," Jay shook his head. "We got it. We're just gonna make something to eat, then go play X-box until dinner."

"Yeah," Ash chimed in with an energetic nod and a big smile. "Do you have any of that chicken salad you make? The one with the grapes and nuts in it, Aunt K?"

"Sure do," she nodded, pulling out the chair between Rayne and Grace. Pointing over her shoulder as she sat down, she added, "Second shelf of the fridge in the glass bowl with the purple lid."

"Oh, yeah," Ash hummed with excitement. "That's the ticket. I do so love that fruity chicken salad."

"And I'm gonna have some of your extra special queso and chips," Ang chimed in, reaching around his twin to grab the yellow bowl covered in hand-painted peppers with a green lid that had become the official queso bowl when the boys were little. "Aunt Kyn, you add all the good stuff to make it just hot enough that I need water after a few chips but not so spicy that it makes my eyes water. I love it."

"I swear, I feed them at home," Grace chuckled, shaking her head as she put sweetener in her coffee. "They keep tellin' me that I'm a good cook but never fail to remind me that Auntie Kyndel makes the best snack food in the world."

"Amen!" Jay cheered. With a double thumbs up and a wink, he went on, "Momma, you can cook anything and everything and it is all awesome, but when you get started on the munchies and the sweets, it's just heaven."

Pretending to swoon as he got the canister of Chex Mix/Gorp, Kyndel's heart was full to bursting when her boy blew a kiss in her direction and said, "Yeah, man, that's my momma right there. I just love that woman."

"Well, you gotta throw some of that love up to Granny Masterson. She taught me to make Chexy Gorp when I was just a little girl."

Looking up, Jay blew a kiss, "Thanks, Granny!" Then dropping his gaze, he threw everything he had Kyndel's way with an added, "I looooooove, my momma."

"Yeah, as long as she's feeding you," Rayne chuckled. Then, holding out his hand, he added, "You are definitely a chip off the old block. Now, before you disappear to your room, eat all the good stuff out of there, and leave me with the wheat Chex and hazelnuts, how about you share some of that yummy mix with your dear, old dad?"

With a twinkle in his eye and more than a hint of a mischievous grin on his face, Jay slowly walked to his dad. Putting a single M&M in his hand, he dashed towards the stairs as fast as his newfound Enchanted speed would allow.

Out of his chair and moving faster than Kyndel could track, Rayne blocked the archway, held out his hand, and said, "Pay the toll, Son."

Laughter once again filled the house as Jay started counting out Chex cereal, M&Ms, mixed nuts, pretzels, and Reese's pieces like they were legos. Before he could get as far as ten pieces, her hubby, the Commander of the MacLendon Force of the Golden Fire Clan, snatched the canister and spun around so quickly that he was nothing but a blur.

Moving one way then the other, always blocked by his dad, Jay yelled, "Mom! Dad's eating all the Chexy Gorp! HELP!"

Laughing so hard it took a second for her to catch her breath, Kyndel threw up her hands in mock surrender, beaming, "Leave me outta this."

"Aww, Mom," Jay pretended to whine. "He's takin' it all. Make him stop!"

Watching as her hubby filled his free hand with as much of the yummy mixture as he could, she pretended to whisper, "There's another canister in the back of the pantry, my love."

Laughing out loud as Rayne shoved the half-full container into his son's outstretched hands, did an abrupt about-face and went straight to the pantry; the tears rolled down her face, and she once again could barely catch her breath when Jay ran up the stairs yelling, "Thanks, Mom! You're the best!"

"Thanks, Aunt K!" Ash called over his shoulder, right on Jay's heels.

"You're the best, Aunt Kyn!" Ang added as the boys disappeared, already teasing each other about who was the best at whatever video game they were about to play.

"I promise, I do feed them," Grace repeated.

"It wouldn't matter how much food we had in both houses plus the kitchen in the Grand Hall. Those boys would still eat us out of house and home, and if there was anything for dessert," Kyndel reassured.

"Seriously, Aaron and I could empty the fridge in an afternoon when we were that age," Aidan snorted. "Used to drive mom and dad crazy."

"Somethings never change," Grace teased.

"For real," Kyndel nodded. Then, turning to face her hubby, she insisted, "Now, spill, Big Man. What's up with Lance and Sam?"

Huffing out a long-suffering breath, his eyes swirled

with silver and gold flecks. "Let me start with, you are gonna get to say 'I told you so, and I am gonna have to say…'"

"You are gonna have to say, 'yeah, you did,' because Sam and Lance know that Sydney is back, she's a grown woman, and she knows who her Mate is."

"You know, there are times when I wonder if your 'spidey senses' are stronger than mine," Grace commented with awe.

"I don't think they are," Kyndel answered without turning away from her Mate. "I just know this hunka-hunka-hot stuff better than I know myself."

"It does make conversations like this easier," Rayne nodded. "And there are times–like this one–when you're only half right, which is fun for me."

Shaking in her chair, her knees bouncing and her hands clenched together so tightly that her knuckles were white, Kyndel made it precisely two seconds before she blurted out, "Tell me. Tell me. Tell me before I just run over there and find out for myself."

Shaking his head and silently chuckling, Rayne winked at his Mate and, as usual, told her everything he knew. "Sam doesn't know that Sydney's back for sure, but she's been having dreams. Lance woke up, and Sam wasn't in bed. He raced around looking for her and found her sleepwalking down the hall. Not wanting to wake her up, he followed her into Syd's old room, watched as she sat on the bed, and hummed *The Bedtime Song*."

"When she awakened," Aidan picked up where Rayne had stopped. "She said, 'Our girl is coming home.' Of course, Lance had no clue what to do, so he went to Siobhan. That's when our resident Healer and all-around amazing woman told him that it was just pregnancy hormones getting the best of her."

"He was nice and thanked her, but our boy isn't buying it," Rayne finished, forcing out another breath and shaking his head. Then, looking right at Kyndel, he added, "It took a bit, but we got him calmed down and headed back home. I told him you would be over tomorrow to hang out with Sam. I hope that's okay."

"Of course," Kyndel quickly agreed. "Is that all?"

"Well, no, is anything in our world ever that easy?" Not waiting for an answer, he went on, "We were finally almost to the truck when we ran into Siobahn, and…"

"Let me guess," Kyndel cut in. "She was less than thrilled that she had to lie, and told you–in her famous mother-knows-best tone–to handle it before she does."

"You got it in one, *Mo ghrá*." Sighing again, his eyes turned a dark purple, almost the color of the Gladioluses in front of Granny's house. "So, go ahead and say it,"

"Nope," Kyndel shook her head. "Not gonna do it."

"You're not?"

"No, I am not," she reiterated. "But I am gonna say what I said when Carrick told us about seeing Sydney in Antarctica with Lore, Sable, and the rest of the Paladins. We need to tell Sam and Lance everything and let them make the decision whether to contact their daughter or not."

"Yes, but…"

Holding up her hand before interrupting her Mate, Kyndel nodded in his direction and then looked at Grace and Aidan before turning back. "You're going to say that Sydney told Carrick she and Shavon, the First Elder, an Ancient One of the Highest Order and one of the Head of the Council of Oracles, had things they had to do before Syd could come home. Now, I completely understand that she has a Most High Calling, has spent time with the Ancients in the Other Realm, or whatever that place is called, and has things that only *she* can do, but these are her parents, and they need to know that she's back."

Sitting up as tall as her five-foot-five-inch frame would allow, Kyndel rolled her shoulders back and, with the authority of someone who understood how important family was, declared, "Sam needs to know that she's not going crazy. And what about Lance? Has he had any dreams? Is his Dragon King talking to him? Has he...?"

"I don't think he's got anything on his mind except making sure that Sam is okay and their baby is happy and healthy when he or she makes their grand appearance."

"Well, I understand that," Kyndel agreed. "But just as sure as God made little green apples, that man has some inkling that there is more to his wife's dreams than just pregnancy hormones." Throwing her hands in the air, she huffed, "Pregnancy hormones? Really? What was Siobhan thinking?"

"She was thinking that the Leader of her Clan, a man, a Dragon who is almost as old as Time, who she respects, who was her husband's best friend, asked her to keep a confidence and to do just that, she had to be less than honest, which..."

"Which is not her style."

Leaning over, Rayne kissed her cheek, smiled, and whispered, "That's my Mate, always on the ball."

"Thanks, Hun, I truly appreciate it, but I think..."

The sound of the doorbell cut off whatever Kyndel was about to say. Instead, she furrowed her brow as she got to her feet and wondered aloud, "Who the heck could that be? Nobody ever rings the bell. Hell. Nobody even knocks. They just holler, 'Hey, I'm here.'"

"And there's only a few people who use the front door," Rayne added.

"That too," she agreed, heading out of the kitchen and through the family room. Hand on the knob, she pulled open the door and stopped short.

Looking at a man that her Granny would've called a long, tall drink of water, complete with a tawny-colored Stetson, Wrangler jeans that fit like a glove, and cowboy boots that had to come from the great state of Texas, she blurted out, "Well, you're a Dragon but not from around here, and that can only mean you're lookin' for my hubby." Stepping back, she motioned toward the family room with a flourish of her free hand that would've made Vanna White proud. "Come on in. Everybody's in the kitchen."

"Thank you, ma'am."

"It's just Kyndel," she chuckled. Closing the door, she asked, "Where in Texas are you from?"

"Damn, you're as good as they said."

"Okay, you're a MacAllen, aren't you?"

"Yes, ma..., I mean, yes, Kyndel, I am." Taking off his hat, he smoothed his dark, wavy hair and added, "Name's Caspian MacAllen, but everybody just calls me Cass. Being named after a god of the Sea has never gotten me anything but a hard time."

"Sounds about right." Turning, she waved for him to follow and talked as she walked. "Well, Cass, welcome to the Golden Fire Lair." Stopping in the archway leading to the kitchen, she smiled when her hubby stood up and continued, "This is my Mate, Rayne."

Waiting until they were done shaking hands, she went on as her Mate stepped to her side and turned toward their friends. Pointing toward the others, she said, "The raven-haired beauty over there is Grace Kensington-O'Brien, and the hunk looking like he might breathe fire is her Mate..."

"Aidan O'Brien," Cass finished her sentence. Nodding to

Grace, he held out his hand to Aidan, explaining as they shook, "I've heard a lot about you. Uncle Owen and Uncle John have told me stories about all of you..." He turned to Rayne and smiled. "...since I was a little boy."

"Well, hell." Shrugging as he chuckled and looked at Rayne, Aidan went back to the MacAllen Dragon and added, "Don't believe everything you hear."

"Trust me," Cass nodded. "I only believe about half of what they tell me. You know us MacAllens, we have a gift for telling good stories."

"That you do," Rayne agreed.

"Can I get you something to drink? To eat?" Kyndel asked.

"No, ma'am, I'm good, but thank you very much."

"Well, have a seat, and tell us why you're here," Rayne suggested.

Looking confused, Cass's brow furrowed as he clenched the brim of his hat. Finally, just when Kyndel was about to ask what was happening, he stuttered, "Umm...I-I guess... That is to say..." Unclenching one of his hands, he ran his fingers through his hair, causing some of the curls to stand on end. "Well, hell, I guess Uncle Owen didn't get around to calling."

"Nope, haven't talked to that old Dragon for at least a month."

Blowing out a sharp breath, he continued, "Okay, Reader's Digest version, I was contacted by Bain, the Leader of the Order of the Brotherhood."

"The who?" Kyndel asked, feeling one of her eyebrows arch on its own accord.

"The Dragon Doctors," Rayne explained. "The ones who..."

"Oh, yeah, you told me about those guys," she nodded,

instantly comforted by the fact that she might actually know what was going on around her. "They're the ones who travel all over the world, go places the CDC, the WHO, and all the other crazy organizations with initials instead of names can't get into. They stop diseases that nobody knows about from spreading and killing everyone in their path."

"Yes, ma'am," Cass nodded. "That's them."

Giving the Dragon a quick frown, she snickered when he blushed the prettiest pink against his tanned cheeks and reassured, "It's okay. I was raised in the South. I know good manners are second nature. You can call me anything you want, not just late for dinner."

"Thank you."

"Now," Rayne cleared his throat. "What does Bain have to do with you showing up on my doorstep?"

"Well, sir, you see, Bain called and said I needed to get over here to see y'all. He said that a woman, someone from y'all's past, was about to come home, and with her, she was bringing..."

But no one heard what Cass said next. Before he could even take a breath, two very important things happened. (1) Lance's voice blasted through the mental link every Dragon in the MacLendon Force and all their Mates shared. Not only was he roaring, but he was pretty obviously losing his ever-loving mind as he bellowed, *The baby is coming! The baby is coming NOW!"*

And (2) Sydney Kavanaugh, in all her glory, walked in through the backdoor, fell into the first available chair, and said, "Hi, y'all! Anybody seen my missing Mate?" Pushing the blond curls out of her face, she gathered the long tresses into a messy bun, wrapped it in a bright red scrunchie, and added, "You know, the one who's been in a coma for four years or so?"

Shocked to see that what everyone had told her was true–the little girl who'd left their Clan about five years prior, when she was just five or six years old, looked to be twenty-nine or thirty–Kyndel still would've known the little cutie anywhere. It wasn't just her blonde curls and brilliant blue eyes that made her so easily recognizable. It was the fact the unconditional love and adoration that only comes from being part of a true family flowed between them just as easily as it had the first time she'd laid eyes on the young lady.

Born of two humans, descendants of the original Mages, Sydney was something special, and not just because she had a magnetic personality. She was the embodiment of the last full-blooded female Dragon born of a King and Queen.

Crossing the room, Kyndel bent down, wrapped her arms around Sydney's shoulders, hugged with all she was worth, and replied, "No, I haven't seen your Mate. As a matter of fact, I thought he was still with the Blue Thunder Clan."

"Yeah," Sydney scoffed with a shake of her head. "I did, too."

"Well, you need to..."

"*I said,*" Lance once again telepathically roared. "The baby is coming!"

Both Kyndel and Sydney sprung upright, but it was the younger woman who squealed, "Wait?! Momma's about to..."

"Yes, Hun," Kyndel nodded, grabbing Syd's hand. "Sam's about to have your little brother or sister! Come on, Sweet-heart. As usual, we've got perfect timing around here. What a better time for one helluva family reunion."

"Well, hot damn!" Sydney jumped to her feet with a

smile and fist pump. "This might just be a Merry Christmas after all."

Following everyone out the door, she added, "Who's the cowboy? Do Mom and Dad know he's coming?"

"No," Cass answered. "Haven't met them yet, but I might be able to help."

"How's that?" Rayne asked.

"I just happen to be a doctor–of both the Dragon and the human variety."

"Well, get a move on, Hoss. If I know my mom, she's tryin' to do it all herself!" Not turning around, she added, "Oh, yeah, she's a doctor, too."

"Lead the way," Cass agreed. "I don't mind pitchin' in, especially since I think you just might know the woman I'm lookin' for."

"And the Christmas surprises just keep comin'," Kyndel whooped, jumping off the back steps and hitting the ground running.

1

"Come out. Come out wherever you are," the sing-songing voice of her friend danced upon the breeze as it blew through the canyon.

Trying with all her might not to laugh out loud, she tightly clenched her lips as her shoulders bounced up and down, and her whole body vibrated with excitement. It was so hard not to giggle and give away her location, but she was determined to win this round of their favorite game.

"I know you're here, Abigail Annabelle Addams." Stopping right before the low-hanging branches of a rather large Texas Madrone tree bopped her in the head, the blond curls flowing from the crown of her head floated like fairy wings as she snapped her head from side to side. "Don't make me pull out the big wand. You won't like it if I pull out the big wand."

"You say that crap all the time," Abbie teased. "Like you need a wand." Chuckling, she threw her voice to the other side of McKittrick Creek, hoping to keep her friend guessing. "I can feel your Magic from a mile away, and you're not even using it. A wand would be a waste of Ashwood and space."

"Ha! I got you now." Sydney Kavanaugh, the closest thing Abbie had to a best friend, barked with laughter. "You messed up and gave me a clue. You're a mile away, aren't ya'? You just told me to meet you here to keep me on my toes, didn't you?"

"I didn't say that."

Teleporting to one of the top branches of an ancient Maple tree, she ended up about seventy feet in the air and loved every minute of it. She could see the land she loved for miles, and best of all, Syd would never think to look up.

Another flash and she was fifty yards closer and a few feet higher. Kneeling on the thick, sturdy limb, she took cover among the dense, brilliantly colored red, yellow, and brown leaves and tried to object, "I said..."

"You said that you could sense me from a mile away, therefore..."

"Therefore, you put two and two together and came up with fourteen."

"Ha. Ha. Ha." Stopping short, the curvy blond propped her left hand on her hip, rolled her eyes, and shook her head. Then, with a twinkle in her bright blue eyes, she teased, "Like I said, don't make me pull out my big girl wand. You know I'll do it, 'cause of how much I hate to lose."

"Like I said, you don't need-nor do you have a wand. And I know how much you hate to lose, but no matter what, you always play fair. So, buckle up, Buttercup. We're about to have some fun."

Standing up, she once again thanked the Great Creator and all The Powers That Be for her short stature. Being just barely five feet tall definitely had its advantages. She never understood why so many of her friends wanted to be taller.

Abbie loved being shorter than the average bear. Not only could she hide in places others wouldn't fit, but she also rarely bumped her head when she was exploring treacherous terrain and scouting locations for one of her many photo shoots. Getting the perfect shot had always been the goal, and there wasn't much that stopped her.

From the moment her dad's mom, Grandma Mary, put a camera in her hand to help with the overwhelming grief of losing her parents, Abbie knew it was what she was meant to do. Through the lens of that Leica, the best camera money could buy at the time, and with the Enchantment she'd inherited from both her mom and dad, the world literally came to life.

She'd been asked to take pictures for the yearbook at school, and that had been fun. Portraits were okay, and candid shots could be fun because teenagers were such goofballs.

But her passion was always in the beautiful sites of the great outdoors.

Whether it was a landscape featuring the yellow blossoms of the Guadalupe violets that only grew on the vertical cliff faces she'd seen every day of her life or the Rainbow trout jumping and splashing in McKitterick Creek, that was where she wanted to be. Those were the images she wanted to share with the world. Everyone needed to see how special things could be outside their little bubbles.

She'd captured the stunning sight of a tornado tearing a path through the Chihuahuan Desert and even gotten a shot of the massive, lumbering, yet still incredibly elusive, Mexican Gopher Tortoise digging a hole on the apron of her burrow to lay her eggs. The subjects she sought out and the pictures she took spoke not only to her heart but also immortalized the beauty and majesty of things most people would never see. They told the story of the land she loved and the beauty that could be found if a person slowed down, took a deep breath, and realized the gifts of the Great Creator, the Universe, God with a capital G, and all The Powers That Be had given them when those incredible Beings breathed life into the big blue and green ball all living beings called home.

At eighteen, she ventured off the Reservation after being accepted into the very prestigious Photography program at the New York Institute of Photography. She would always remember the day she got the letter. It had been the surprise of a lifetime, and she would spend her life thanking her Grandmother for it.

The squeak of the screen door as she pulled it open always made her smile. No matter what kind of day she'd had, that sound told her that she was home. Most thought she smiled because she and Grandma Mary had forgotten to buy WD40 so often that it had become a joke amongst all their friends and family, but they couldn't have been more wrong.

That whine of aluminum rubbing against aluminum said, 'You've done it. You're in your happy place, Abbie Addams.' And the genuine, heartfelt happiness came when Marilyn, the mixed breed Chow Chow she'd rescued ten years earlier, raced down the long, galley-like breezeway with a twinkle in her eye and so much unconditional love in her heart that it made her golden and auburn fur shine in the fading rays of the sun.

The breezeway, sort of like a sun porch, was narrow and long, with windows on one side to let the beautiful sunlight in to wash away the shadows. Behind those windows that were a bugger to wash, there were screens.

Grandma threw open the windows at the first warm breeze, letting the cool winds carry in the glorious aroma of the bluish violet Gayfeathers and bright red blossoms of the Cardinal flowers from the Guadalupe Mountains. It was glorious and just one of the many perks of living on the Res.

Opposite the windows were knotty pine panels that had been put over the red brick to allow for decorating. Of course, Grandma Mary had hung hooks for coats and jackets, made rows of short steps from the hardwood of a fallen tree for muddy boots, and collected loads of mismatched, eclectic furniture that somehow all fit together just the way she wanted them to. That porch or breezeway or whatever anyone wanted to call it became the unofficial welcoming room for any and all who came to visit pretty much the day after it was built, and it was Abbie's favorite place in the whole house.

"I'm home, Grandma," she called out. "It's my turn to cook. Whatcha want for dinner?" Not waiting for an answer, she kept right on going. "I was thinkin' we could try out that new brick oven the MacAllen boys built. Doesn't a homemade pizza sound ah-mazing? I've been thinking about it all day."

"Anything works for me," Grandma answered, sunshine in her voice. "But first, you need to come here. I've got something important to show you."

Furrowing her brow as she ruffled Marilyn's fur, Abbie whispered, "What is she up to, Girl?"

Grumbling, her version of talking, the Chow Chow mix rubbed her nose in Abbie's outstretched palm, looking for the treats she knew were in the young woman's pockets. "Yeah, well, I have no clue what you said, but you can have your cookies anyway. I know you've been waitin' all day."

Tossing one of the heart-shaped treats into the air, she clapped and cheered when Marilyn jumped so high her feet left the ground and snatched the treat between her teeth. "There ya' go! That's my girl."

Loving that her furry friend yipped and danced on her hind feet after devouring the treat, Abbie handed the pup another and headed toward the doorway into the kitchen. *Stopping when both feet were barely over the threshold, she couldn't believe her eyes.*

Inhaling sharply, she held her breath while taking in the most extensive array of camera equipment she'd ever seen anywhere other than the Photo and Hobby Shop on Mills Avenue in downtown Valentine. From a first-rate leather bag with a crossbody strap, to lenses of every variety, to a tripod so new she'd only seen it in a trade magazine, there was so much stuff she didn't know where to start.

Gaze flying to her Grandmother's, she breathed, "What is...? How did you...? I can't even..."

"You can't even finish a sentence?" *Grandma Mary laughed, her smoky voice so filled with love and adoration that Abbie's heart skipped a beat.* "You're at a loss for words? Wow! That's a first."

Before she could ask the matriarch of the Addams Family what was happening, the older woman was off her stool and across the room with a smile so bright it rivaled the sun over Guadalupe Peak. Handing her an envelope, she ordered in the most loving way, "Open that thing before I lose my mind. Even though I know..." *She tapped her temple with the tip of the index finger of her free hand.* "...what it says, I still need to see it in black and white."

Doing as she was told without the slightest hesitation, Abbie tore into the envelope, pulled out the tri-folded paper, and with a flourish that rivaled Indiana Jones' crack of a whip, she had the fancy, embossed stationary flat on the counter in less than a minute.

It took several starts and three complete readings of the letter before she looked up at her Grandmother in complete shock. "But how can this be? I didn't..."

"You didn't have to," *Mary Addams proudly announced.* "I did it. I put together your portfolio, filled out the application, and *even got letters of recommendation from your teachers, Principal Shultz, and the Mayor himself.”*

“But how did you know…?”

“Darlin, haven't you learned by now that nothin' gets past me?”

Opening her mouth, not sure what was going to come out, Abbie was almost happy when her grandma once again cut her off. “I promised your momma and daddy that I would take care of you. From the day your momma found out she was pregnant, all those two ever talked about was wanting the best for you. They wanted to make all your dreams come true. They…” Stopping as her voice cracked, Grandma Mary inhaled deeply, smiled the smile Abbie had come to count on, and exhaled.

Running her fingers through the tight salt and pepper curls atop her head, she nodded, “Kari and Andrew wanted you to be proud of your heritage, to accomplish all your dreams, and to be whatever your little heart desired—no matter what that happened to be.” Moving closer, she laid her hand on Abbie's shoulder. “They are looking down from the Heavens with such pride. Can you feel it? I know I can.”

“Yes, Grandma, I sure can feel them.” Closing the scant distance between them, Abbie pushed up on her toes and hugged Mary with everything she had.

Pulling back when Marilyn whined and pushed between them, she knew her eyes were full of unshed tears as she looked at Grandma and confidently professed, “Thank you so very much. I'm gonna make all of you so proud.”

“Oh, darlin', you already do that every day, in every way.”

Forcing herself out of one of her happiest memories, Abbie walked as close to the end of the branch as she dared. Smiling down at Sydney, it was all she could do not to laugh out loud. The poor dear was looking everywhere but up. She used tiny bits of her immense Magic to delve under rocks, piles of fallen leaves, and even into the creek. Sadly, nothing worked, and she got more frustrated every time she came up empty-handed.

"Time to make my grand entrance," Abbie whispered to herself. "And claim the victory once and for all."

Still cloaked by the thick foliage and a good amount of the Nûññë'hï Enchantment that filled her heart and soul, Abbie floated to the ground. The second her feet touched the Fluff Grass growing on the banks of the McKittrick Creek, she let go of the Magic keeping her invisible from her friend, stuck out her tongue, then happily teased, "Nanny-nanny-booboo, I got you!"

"Yes!" Sydney laughed. "I do so love that trick. I don't even care that you beat me. I just love when you do that, and someday you're gonna have to teach me."

Leaning forward, Abbie waggled her eyebrows and, in a conspiratorial whisper, teased, "I could teach you, but then I'd have to kill ya'. You know how us Little People are."

Unable to hold back her laughter any longer, she loved that her bestie thought her joke was just as funny as she did. Their goofy sense of humor was just one of the many things they had in common. From the first time they'd met, Abbie and Sydney made each other laugh so hard that they had tears running down their faces and were gasping for air. It was always a party every time they were together.

Waiting until their last case of giggles dwindled, Abbie tried to get tough, and with her best Brenda Lee Johnson impression, she questioned, "Okay, give it up. What the hell are you doing all the way out here when your momma just gave birth to your baby sister? I mean, yes, the Chihuahuan Desert and the Res, well, pretty much all of Texas, is God's country, but what the heck? I can't even imagine how you got away without Lance tying you to a chair while Sam cheered him on as she threw questions at you like they were bullets from a Tommy gun. The little bit I know about your momma says that she would want a blow-by-blow account of the last ten years of your life."

Chuckling all over again, Sydney shook her head and bumped her elbow into Abbie's as they turned toward the path to the Reservation and started walking. "It was nothing like that." Her shoulders slumped, and her voice took on an almost haunted tone. "They didn't even know I was there."

"They what?!" Stopping mid-step, Abbie spun to the left. Gently grabbing her friend's upper arm, she turned the blonde and added, "How did you accomplish that? What happened? Are you okay?"

"I didn't accomplish anything. Something weird happened. Really, really weird. Mind-blowing even." Inhaling deeply, she assured, "Yes, I'm fine. Thanks for askin', kiddo.

"Well, it had to be oh-my-God weird and then some for you not to, at the very least, see your mom, dad, and new sister. Spill, Girl. Spill! I'm 'bout to bust over here. My mind is workin' overtime, and nothin' it's comin' up with is good."

"I'm spillin'," Syd sighed. Then, to let her buddy know she was irritated with herself and not her, she quickly added, "And you're right, it was oh-my-God weird and then some."

Nodding toward the large rocks on the banks of the creek, the blond slowly put one foot in front of the other, and Abbie slipped into step beside her. Patience was never something the Photographer possessed, unless it had to do with getting the perfect picture and it was even worse when she was nervous or knew someone she cared about was in pain. It was all she could do not to ball up her fists, pump them in the air, and yell, "Just put me out of my misery and tell me what happened so I can come up with a way to make you feel better."

Thankfully, she didn't have to lose her mind or her self-respect because, at that moment, Sydney started to explain. "Halfway to their house–*our house*–with all the guys from dad's Force, all their Mates, and pretty much every other Dragon, human, and everybody else in the whole Clan racing with us, my feet just stopped. They simply refused to move. I was stuck in place with everybody zoomin' past me, and there wasn't a damn thing I could do about it."

"What the hell? Was it…?"

"Nope, it wasn't Magic of any kind, not Black, not White, not anywhere in between," Syd answered even before Abbie finished. "It was like nothing I've ever felt before–good, bad, or ugly." Pushing the curls on the right side of her face behind her ear, she looked out at the stream as it rushed by and finally picked up where she'd left off. "I was just about to yell for help when my heart skipped about four beats, and it took everything in me just to draw a single breath. It was like I'd been gut punched by some invisible force, and there wasn't a darn thing I could do."

Bending at the waist, she plucked a flowering weed from the ground and fiddled with the petals. "I even had spots dancing before my eyes like I got one time when I flew too high with one of the Oracles. I knew something wasn't right, but I also knew Mom and Dad and the baby needed everyone more than I did." Audibly inhaling then exhaling, she added, "To make things even weirder, it was like no one saw me standing there. No one stopped to ask what was wrong? Not even the guy, one of the MacAllen Dragons who was at Rayne and Kyndel's. They just ran past me without so much as a sideways glance."

"Okay," Abbie drew out the word, unsure what else to say.

Smiling as her friend slid her eyes to the right, looking at her through her long, dark eyelashes, the Photographer added with a snicker she hoped would ease her friend's troubled heart, "Besides, if you had been in real trouble, Shavon or one of the other Oracles or Special Beings or *whoever* lives up there in the Citadel would've come flashing out of the Other Realms and saved your booty, right?"

"Yeah," Sydney nodded, her eyes getting back some of their usual luster. "I thought of that after the fact." Snorting a sarcastic laugh, she continued, "But in the moment, I was freakin' out, then I heard Garrett's voice."

"Like Garrett-Garrett? Your...?" Jumping to her feet, her finger moved between them so quickly that it was little more than a blur. "...Mate? The one man made for you by the Universe? Your hunka-hunka...."

"...burnin' love Dragon Man?" Syd chuckled, and that made Abbie snicker. "Yep, that's the only Garrett we know."

The Photographer couldn't stop the wheezing laughter that slipped from her lips. Hunka-hunka-burnin' love was what she called her Fated Mate because she didn't know his name. She knew absolutely nothing about him except that when he wanted to, the dude could sprout wings and scales and blow flames in every direction.

It was exasperating at best and downright irritating if she thought about it too long. Just like everything that came along with being a Supernatural Being, there was mystery, intrigue, and a stark lack of hard evidence to put to anything. All she knew for sure was what she'd been told by one of the three Nûññë'hï who appeared on her twenty-first birthday.

Thankfully, she'd known they were coming–not a definite time, but the date was as good as written in stone. It was more than legend. It was a fact, and for that, she was grateful. However, what bothered her more than a little bit was that out of everything important the Nûññë'hï said, all the instructions they gave, the only tidbit they dropped about her Mate, the man made for her by the Universe and the Great Creator, was that he was a Dragon Shifter, one of the Universe's Chosen Warriors, a Dragon Guardsman.

Sure, she'd begged, badgered, and tried to outsmart the Nûññë'hï, but it got her absolutely nowhere. Those Immortal Beings, known as The People Who Will Live Forever by the Cherokee Nation, were more tight-lipped than Santa and his Elves the day before Christmas–which also just happened to be Abigail Annabelle Addams's birthday.

Being born on Christmas Eve wasn't all it was cracked up to be. She just thanked the Heavens that her parents hadn't given her a hokey, holiday-themed name. That would've been too much to handle and not befitting the Nûññë'hï she found out she was destined to be.

Likened to the Fairies of the English world, the Nûññë'hï were so much more to those blessed to carry the Blood of the Cherokee Ancestors within them. They were the Benevolent Ones. They cared for the lost and wandering, guiding them safely home from wherever they happened to be. They also protected the people forced to relocate to other lands and safeguarded them from harm.

The coolest thing was, for the most part, the Nûññë'hï stayed invisible. If, by some miracle or the need of those they were assisting, they had to be seen, they always resembled the person they appeared to–in most cases, pretty much every case, it was a member of the Cherokee Nation or a relative.

When Abbie first realized that she'd inherited the heart and soul of the Nûññë'hï from her mom, she could not have been happier. Not only was she one of The People Who Would Live Forever, but she finally understood where her love of nature, music, and dancing had come from and why she possessed the unquenchable desire to spread happiness everywhere she went. Oh, and it also shed light on her need to protect life in all its many forms and help anyone and everyone in need who crossed her path. It was as if her eyes had been opened, and she'd been introduced to another side of herself–an important side.

Of course, the Nûññë'hï had given her some parting advice and ended with, "When the time is right, you will understand everything we could not tell you. Be happy, *A-da-ge-yu-di*, for you are more special than you can ever imagine."

Being called 'beloved one' in the Cherokee language had been sweet, but did they have to make everything a riddle? Thankfully, it wasn't long before Abbie understood at least a little bit of her destiny.

Less than a week after the three Nûññë'hï visited, she had a dream that further portrayed the importance of The Immortal Ones, The People Who Would Live Forever. It also explained why, even though Abigail Annabelle Addams was a true member of the Cherokee Nation, she had a beautiful mane of long red hair. The dream had been so real, so vivid, that she never forgot the feel of the cool, dry breeze of the desert on her cheeks or the way the soft cotton of her gown wrapped around her legs.

Brushing the tangles of long, auburn curls from her face, Abbie looked upon the battleground she'd visited many times. However, on this occasion, it was very different. There was no wrought iron fence, no plaques paying homage to the brave men and women who'd lost their lives, and no bronze statues of the Timber Wolves and Dragons who had fought alongside those of the Thorntree Tribe to protect their lands, their home, and their people.

No, on this fateful night, one lone woman stood in the center of what had originally been a pasture. Facing her were at least twenty figures surrounded in an evil, malevolent, swirling fog that obscured some of the long, grotesque shadows they cast.

From her place on the sidelines, Abbie could just barely make out the true silhouette of the leader. Ten feet tall if he was an inch, jagged, misshapen horns jutted from either side of his head. His nose and mouth formed a ghoulish snout, but it was the thick, pitted tusks jutting from his bottom lip and curving until their steely points almost touched the rotting flesh beneath his eyes that gave her pause.

Then, a viscous blob of horrific goo dripped from those massive tusks. Everything moved in slow motion. Abbie's heart stopped, and the breath was frozen in her lungs as the globule that glowed a fluorescent green in the moonlight fell to the ground.

The smattering sizzle broke the spell. Everything moved at the speed of sound. The blob exploded like an atomic bomb. A mushroom cloud filled the air with noxious fumes. The dark, dense, almost impenetrable smoke spread like wild fire. It was everywhere.

And that was when all Hell really broke lose.

The leader threw back his head. His bottom jaw unhinged, falling onto the scarred and disfigured flesh of his enormous chest. Fire, brimstone, and ash flew from his lips, reigning down and torching every living thing as his battle cry ripped through the airwaves.

Dropping his head, the monster—that's the only name she

could think to call him–raised the staff, topped with a contorted skull, high in the air. Waiting for a single beat of her heart, the bastard's head snapped to the side.

Spearing her with a look so evil she felt it in every fiber of her being, his crimson eyes glowed, blood flowing from their depths as he growled, "Kill them all!"

Everything happened so fast that it took years for Abbie to piece it all together. The Skeenah, as she found out they were called, Shifted into all sorts of mismatched, animated creatures from the depths of the Underworld. They advanced on the single female Warrior still standing tall in the middle of the battlefield. Their hate–a living, breathing entity Abbie felt in the depths of her soul–drove them faster and faster. Even the most hideous of them, the ones with the most unrelated, mutilated parts, ran so fast they were impossible to track.

Unable to scream, her mouth was opened so wide that her jaws ached. There simply was no sound, no mist from her breath, absolutely nothing as she tried with all her might to warn the beautiful Ditlihi–Chosen Warrior– to move... to act... to do anything to save her own life.

Just as the Skeenah were about to descend upon her, a bright, white light filled every atom, every particle, every molecule of absolutely everything. In the blink of an eye, in every square foot of the battlefield, stood a Cherokee Warrior. Ditlihi one and all, they moved together like a well-oiled machine. Their formations were perfection. It was instinctual. Each knew what all the others were doing without so much as a glance or a thought.

Surrounding the Skeenah, the Ditlihi never drew a weapon, never raised a hand, and never said a word. The only movement they made was a single nod and one solitary stomp of their right foot.

The ground beneath the feet of the Skeenah opened into the

biggest, deepest crater she could ever imagine. Flames shot into the air. Tentacles, dripping with black, oily, fetid blood, slithered and slid from the hole, wrapping around the Demons until they were nothing more than undulating, variegated flesh.

In one coordinated effort, the tentacle constricted. The blood-curdling howls of agony and torment attacked her ears as whatever unholy essence had animated them was squeezed from their bodies. Pulled into the crater with a single, swift tug, the Skeenah were gone as quickly as they'd appeared.

Eyes snapping to the Ditlihi, she found only the stunning, stoic redhead as a reassuring voice floated through her mind. "Dear Abigail, I feel the Spirit of the Nûññë'hï alive within you and the Soul of the Great Thorntree Timber Wolf standing guard. We are one, A-da-ge-yu-di. Remember this night. Remember this vision. You are the Hope. You are Nûññë'hï."

The snap of fingers pulled Abbie from her thoughts. Eyes meeting her friend's, she immediately grabbed Syd's hands and apologized. "I am so sorry! I don't know what is going on in my brain. That is the second time..."

"That's the second time your memories have taken over when you least expected it and refused to let go until they'd shown you what you didn't know you needed to see."

"Okay." Drawing out the word, she opened her eyes wide. "You didn't ask. You said that like you knew." Squeezing Syd's hand, she added, "So, what gives? What aren't you tellin' me?"

"Well, hold onto your hat, my friend, I may not know much about the People Who Will Live Forever, but after almost ten years with the Oracles, I've picked up a few things. When your memories start talking, demanding to be heard, something big, monumental, life-changing is about to happen, and..."

"And..." Abbie begged and demanded in the same breath."

"And I'm pretty sure I met the Dragon made for you by the Universe."

2

"Okay, start at the beginning," his aunt suggested with the authority of a woman who knew her request would be followed but loved him enough to add a comforting lilt at the end, telling him that he had a special place in her heart. "But give me just a minute. I need some of the good stuff to be sure my bran is firing on all cylinders." Filling her favorite Christmas mug, the one she'd been using for as long as he could remember, his aunt asked over her shoulder, "You want a cup? It's fresh. I'd just poured the water in when you came through the door." With a short gasp, she added, "Oh wait! Are you still off caffeine?"

The chuckle in her voice, the one that had been there since the first time he'd asked for decaf almost three years ago, made the left side of his mouth raise in what some called the 'Cass smirk.' Not only had she made fun of him, but all of his cousins and their Mates had laughed so loud and for so long he almost lost all willpower right then and there. Then Uncle Owen stood up for him, telling all of them to mind their own business, and Cass was instantly more determined than ever.

Of course, that drive only lasted about a year. No caffeine was a hard pill to swallow–or not swallow, as the case was for him. After all, doctors weren't meant to function without coffee. At least not when they worked the kind of hours he did. He could be stitching up bombing victims in some far-off country in the morning, then back to the University of Texas MD Anderson Cancer Center, where he was the lead physician in the research to kick cancer's ass. The human race had enough problems without a fucking disease that attacked without warning and, in most cases, refused to be beaten. He'd always kept a rigorous schedule, but lately, things seemed to be compounding.

Smiling because of all the happy memories being back at the MacAllen Ranch revived within him, even the ones where he was the butt of the joke, and despite the events that had brought him back to South Texas, Cass laughed, "Nope, gave up that battle pretty much as soon as I started."

"Thank the Heavens," cheered Barbara McAllen, his mother's best friend, his surrogate mom, and the Mate of his Uncle Owen. "And I think lasting as long as you did is a testament to your gumption and stubbornness. I just can't figure out why anyone with our metabolism would ever deprive themselves of something they loved as much as I know *you* love your java."

"Well, it was something I tried when I was…"

"When you were havin' trouble sleepin'? I mean, the last time, not the first."

"Yep. I see you remember." Happily snickering, he added, "Well, you pretty much remember everything."

"I do, and sometimes it's a curse, but I like it more than I hate it." Without pausing, she returned to the subject at hand. "So, did you find out caffeine wasn't the problem? It wasn't keepin' you up at night?"

"You know I did."

"Because you went to see Bane, the Leader of the Brotherhood of the Dragons? And that Ancient Healer, Doctor, and Seer was able to tell you why you couldn't get a good night's sleep by sharing what he 'saw'?"

"You know I did, and he did," he repeated with a snort of laughter. "And before you ask another question that you already know the answer to, let me just say, yes, I asked him about my insomnia, along with other things, when I went to see him instead of just calling because you told me I needed to speak to him face to face."

"See?" Turning toward him with two mugs of steaming, wonderfully aromatic coffee, his aunt's special blend, she closed the distance. Placing one in front of him, she stepped back toward the closest chair, sat down, and took a sip of her coffee–never breaking eye contact. "Now, was that so hard?"

"Not at all, Aunt Barb."

"You always were my favorite."

"Yeah, right." He scoffed, unable to contain his smirk. "That's what you say to all of us when we do what you tell us to."

"Works every time." Winking, she took another sip, then set her mug on the table between the bowl of fruit and three loaves of freshly baked bread he was sure had been made because she knew he was coming home. Leaning forward, she laid her left hand on the highly polished wood and grinned. "So, spill, Cass, my love. Confusion and frustration are written all over your face, and I just can't stand when any of my boys get all tangled up in their BVDs."

"Well…" He forced out a long-suffering breath before continuing. "It's like I was trying to say–but failin' miserably–when I walked in. The birth of the babe went off without a hitch. It was the easiest delivery I've ever had. I mean, there were more Doctors, Healers, and Elders in the room than there are at most hospitals these days. We outnumbered everybody else at least two-to-one. Besides, I'm pretty sure Sam could've done it all by herself if Lance hadn't put out the old, mental all–call. As a matter of fact, I'm also pretty sure ..."

"She would've *preferred* to do it herself because then there wouldn't have been an audience?"

"I see you've met her?"

"I have, and I loved her at first sight. I *love* all of them. We may come from different parts of the world and different walks of life, but we're all joined by..."

"We're all joined by one simple belief," Cass reiterated what he'd been told every day of his life for as long as he could remember. "There are no coincidences. The Universe does not make mistakes. Fate will not be denied, and the Great Creator sees us all as Their children. We are one Family under the Sun, Moon, and Stars."

Smiling brightly, her eyes shining with a love that reminded him of his mother and made his heart swell three times its size, just like the Grinch's in his favorite holiday cartoon, she winked. "See? You got it in one."

"Yeah, well, here's the freaky part, the one I was trying to tell you about when I first walked in. The one that has me so confused I'm really not sure which end is up."

"Oh, yes." Sitting back, she crossed her legs, picked up her mug, and with her free hand pointed. "With all the talk of babies, I almost forgot. I really need grandchildren, ya' know that, right?" With a wistful sigh, it only took a second before she was once again focused on him. Clapping, she assured, "But that's a story for another day. Right here and now, I'm all ears. You have my full attention. Tell me what happened that has you so upset."

"It's not that I'm upset." He stopped, ran the fingers of his right hand through his hair–something he only did when he was trying to solve a puzzle or find an elusive answer to a pain-in-the-ass question that refused to leave him alone–and sighed for what seemed like the umpteenth time. "It's more like I'm out of sorts... Confused... Completely out of my depth."

"That just can't be so." Shaking her head, Aunt Barbara uncrossed her legs and sat up so straight it was as if she was a puppet, and someone had pulled her strings. "You are one of the smartest people I've ever met, and that's sayin' something, sir. I've met *a lot* of brilliant people in all my years, a lot of clever Beings with minds like steel traps." Wagging her finger at him in fun, she added, "And if you ask me the number of those years, I will kick ya' in the shin and refuse to feed you."

Hands up in mock surrender, Cass tried not to laugh as he solemnly replied, "No way, no, ma'am. You taught me better than to ever ask a lady her age or her dress size."

"See? You really are my favorite."

"And that's the way I like it," he chuckled.

"Well, it's just because you're so damned smart."

Holding up her hand when Cass was about to interrupt, she kept right on going. "And I do not say that just because you're my nephew by marriage and the son of the best friend I ever had."

She winked and crinkled her nose, an expression that had always made him feel better even when he'd just fallen out of the tree, broken his arm, and bent the wing of the model airplane he'd paid for with the money he'd gotten for his eighth birthday.

"It's because it's true. You were smart as a whip from the day you opened your eyes. There was never a child born who could figure something out faster than you–not even one of my own. Not to mention, you've been a doctor since before your twenty-first birthday and healed and saved people of all shapes and sizes in more places and eras than most. So, if you're flummoxed, well, you better tell me the whole story. Then once we have all the facts, we'll spread them out and connect them one at a time like those blasted million-piece jigsaw puzzles you loved as a kid. Sound good?"

"It does," he readily agreed, truly meaning every word.

There hadn't been a time in his life, even when his parents still walked the Earth, when his Aunt Barbara and Uncle Owen couldn't make him feel better. So, after taking a drink of coffee and accepting a plate of Barbara MacAllen's special peanut butter chocolate chip oatmeal cookies, he started to tell her everything that had happened.

"I got to the Lair of the Golden Fire Clan without a problem. Flew through the night and landed after lunch. I went straight to Commander MacLendon's house and was welcomed just like I was home."

"I told you Kyndel and Rayne were good people."

"Oh, yeah, they are. I knew they had to be, but I'm not afraid to admit that hearing the Southern in Kyndel's voice felt good. She didn't even get mad that I kept calling her ma'am."

"She's good that way."

"She sure is." Pausing for a second to get his thoughts back in order, Cass started again. "So, after I got introduced to everyone, of course, they wanted to know why I was there. I explained that I thought they were expecting me because it's where Bane said I was supposed to be."

Pausing for a spilt-second, he shook his head and gave a quick chuckle. "Well, they were confused, and rightfully so. Uncle Owen hadn't gotten around to calling and telling anyone I was coming. And, apparently, Bane hadn't either."

"I understand Bane not callin' but that husband of mine." She shook her head and smiled. "You just gotta love that Uncle of yours," Barbara chuckled. "I knew I should've done it. I even suggested it, but Owen said he needed to talk to Rayne about something, and it was as good a time as any to get it all taken care of in one call. So..."

"So, you left it up to him."

"Yep, I did."

"Well, it doesn't matter," Cass acquiesced. "I repeated that Bane said I needed to go to the Golden Fire Clan because a woman from *their* past was coming home. I went on to say that she was bringing my Mate with her, and for some reason, I needed to find the woman made for me sooner rather than later."

Stopping, he took another drink of coffee, looked out the window, and, after a few seconds of thinking back over everything that had happened, continued. "I was just about to finish by saying, 'And that is as far as Bane could see into the future,' when Lance yelled that the baby was coming. In the middle of that, their daughter, Sydney, arrived, and we were all runnin' quicker than a cat dances on a hot tin roof across the Lair to help."

"I do love it when your Texas comes shinin' through."

"Well, then you'll love what comes next." Turning so he could look his aunt in the eye, Cass went on, "Two steps out the back door, I realized Sydney was who I needed to talk to. She was the person from the past coming back to her home, the Golden Fire Clan, that Bane saw in his vision. I told my rascally Dragon King, Blár, that we needed to speak with her as soon as we could, and..."

"And I agreed," the Dragon King's voice came out of Cass's mouth without a break or pause in the conversation. They had been together so long that Cass was used to anything his alter ego did and took it all in stride. "Also, I would like to take this time to say a proper hello to you, Barbara Anne Thorntree MacAllen, Luna Wolf of the Thorntree Timber Wolf Pack, Daughter of the Great Chief Cheveyo and Ghigau of the Thorntree Cherokee Nation. It is always such a pleasure to be in the home of 'the One Who Speaks With the Great Spirit.' I have greatly missed our talks and look forward to more."

"It is just great to have you here, King Blár. I, too, have missed our talks, but you have to stop with all the formality. I'm just Barbara MacAllen, or Barb, if you like. I know you and your kin are big on formality, but 'round here, I'm just Barbara, Aunt Barb, or Mom." She chuckled. "However," With a wink and another crinkle of her nose, she got closer and, in a faux conspiratorial whisper, admitted, "It does always do my heart good to be greeted in the old way every once in a while."

"Then I shall strive to always do that for you, *Mo charaid ghràdhach*," the Dragon King answered, the brogue of the Isle of Skye where the Universe had breathed him into existence thick in his voice, before he returned to the back of the Guardsman's soul.

"Well, now, haven't I been put in my place," Cass chuckled. "Sorry about that, Old Man." Then, to his aunt, he also said, "Sorry, I was..."

"You were all consumed with whatever happened at the Golden Fire Lair and didn't think of letting King Blár speak to me." Nodding, she went on, "It's okay. He and I will speak

later. You keep going. I'm on the edge of my seat over here."
Snickering, she added, "Even though I do love that old
Dragon King of yours."

"And he loves you." Another sip of coffee, and Cass
started where he'd left off. "Like I was sayin', we were all
runnin' at top speed through Kyndel's garden and across the
pasture. It reminded me of the All Dragon Games from
when I was a young'un. Anyway, about halfway between the
MacLendon's house and the Clinic, Sydney just
disappeared."

"You mean, she went a different way."

"No," he insisted, "I meant what I said. She. Disappeared." Up on his feet in one fluid motion, Cass spun on
the heels of his boots and started pacing the length of the
massive kitchen that felt more like home than his own ever
had. Without missing a beat, he went on, "One second, she
was running by my side, talking about how she was so
excited to finally see her mom and dad again and to
welcome the new baby, and the next, she wasn't. *Poof!* She
was gone. When we got to the Clinic, I asked a few people
where she'd gone, and they all said they hadn't seen her for
almost ten years since she went to the Refuge in the Citadel
with the Ancient One, Shavon."

Returning to his chair, he sat and grabbed a cookie from
the plate. Using it like the pointer his old anatomy professor,
Dr. Benedict, used to use, he went on, "Of course, my hunt
for Sydney Kavanaugh was cut short when Siobhan Walsh
asked me to assist Charlie O'Brien, another doctor and the
Mate of Aaron O'Brien... With a single, sharp shake of his
head, he added, "Why am I telling you who people are? You
know everybody."

His aunt nodded, and he continued, "Always have.
Always will." He forced a snicker to ease the tension beating

at him from the inside out. "So, Sam was tryin' to hand out directions, do her Lamaze breathing, and shatter every bone in her husband's hand, all while having one contraction on top of another. Happily, for all involved, especially Lance's hand, if the look of utter pain on his face was any indication, the birth didn't take long. The baby was happy and healthy from the start. She literally cried for two seconds, then started cooing and smiling. At twenty-four inches long and eight pounds and twelve ounces with light brown curls, she was the definition of adorable."

"Oh, I love babies, especially the chubby ones," Barbara swooned. "Tell me, did she have thick little thighs and cheeks you just wanted to kiss?"

"Yes, ma'am, she sure did." Smiling, the expression and the memory making him feel a little less frustrated, Cass started to resume his account of what had taken place when his Aunt asked, "What did they name her?"

"Oh, yeah," he snickered. "Orla Elizabeth Anne Kavanaugh."

"What a name. It's perfect."

"I understood Orla because it means Golden Princess. One look and there was no denying that the sweet little girl was most definitely a princess, and we all know her daddy is a golden Dragon, so..." Shrugging, he opened his hands and nodded. "I admit, I was a bit confused about the two middle names, but Kyndel explained that Elizabeth is Sydney's middle name and Anne is Sam's."

"Now, the second she mentioned Sydney, I remembered why I was really there and asked where the young lady had gone, and do you know what, Aunt Barb?"

"I don't, but I'm sure you're gonna tell me."

"You're right. I am." Without so much as a breath, Cass declared, "She shrugged, turned, and walked away."

"And you left it there?"

"Not exactly. I stayed around for another day to be sure Mother and Baby Orla were okay. I absolutely tried to talk to Kyndel again, but she had more excuses than feathers in a henhouse, always sayin' she was so busy but would be right back. As you can imagine, when she came back, she was just as busy. Where everyone was concerned, well, they just looked at me like I had three heads if I even mentioned Sydney's name."

"What about their son, Jay? That beautiful boy nearly talked my ear off the last time I saw him."

"I saw him for about two minutes in total, and that was when he and the O'Brien twins–Angus and Ashton–were raiding the refrigerator and the pantry. Those three were almost as good at eatin' their parents out of house and home as me, Jed, and Gage were at that age. But instead of disappearing out to the barn or the nearest tree or cave, they were busy playin' video games." Taking a drink of coffee, he remembered to say, "I'm sure you already know, but Jay had his first Shift right before Thanksgiving."

"I had heard that," his aunt agreed. "I knew he would be early to embrace the Magic of his Dragon. I bet the O'Brien twins aren't far behind."

"Yeah, Blár and I could feel the Mysticism of the Shift when they were anywhere around. It won't be long."

"Well, good for them." Motioning with her free hand, she asked, "What about Rayne? He's always been a straight shooter. I remember your Uncle Owen asking him about something many years ago. Even though whatever was happening was top secret, the Commander told your Uncle that he couldn't explain at the time but would as soon as he could. We both respected him for that. Then true to his word and his character, he called a week later, after getting permission from the Elders, and answered all our questions."

"I knew Rayne would at the very least tell me to mind my own business, but he was nowhere to be found," Cass explained. "Nether were Aidan or Aaron O'Brien. I asked their Mates when they would be back, and they were as tight-lipped as Kyndel. Now, you know me, I tried to be patient, but I was not blessed with very much of that particular virtue. I know you know how antsy I get when I have something on my mind and have nothing to keep me busy."

"I do, better than most."

"Yeah, well, I just said my goodbyes and thanked everyone so much for their incredible hospitality. I dropped by to check on Sam, Lance, and little Orla and then went to see Bane. Thankfully, he was back in Houston, looking at the results of our latest research."

"How did that go?"

"Well, he liked what he saw with the gene splicing. Just like we suspected, Dragon DNA perfectly integrates with human DNA, and without the Magic of the Ancients and the Universe, there is no chance of them Shifting and becoming a Dragon Sylph. The Heavens know we do not need Elemental Air Dragons with no soul or moral compass roaming the Earth–no matter how much I hate cancer and what it does to the humans."

"Well, that's good news."

"It is." He nodded. "My professional life is going great. As far as my personal life is concerned, well, I tried to catch up with Bane after our meeting at the lab, but as usual, he was gone. So, that's why I'm here. Apparently, he went straight out to the middle of the Chihuahuan..." Throwing his thumb over his shoulder, he continued. "Okay, well, he's out there under the Desert, working with Declan of the Blue

Thunder Clan, the Big Cat Pride, and a few others to remove the frozen creatures from the ice."

"And you're here because...?" She drew out the words while trying not to laugh. Watching the effort, it took his aunt not to let go of a good guffaw, Cass started to chuckle even though he had a cookie in his mouth.

Swallowing the most wonderful confection he'd ever tasted, he took a sip of coffee before answering. "Because it is almost Christmas, your boys are all Mated, and you need help decorating this big old house–inside and out."

"Oh, I see, and you're hoping for an invitation to Christmas Dinner, and since your birthday is the same day, you're thinking there might be a big, ole Texas sheet cake on the dessert table?"

"Absolutely!" Nodding, Cass picked up another cookie. Unlike before, he didn't wave it around. He simply held it between them as he added, "As well as Christmas Eve, Boxing Day, New Year's Eve, New Year's Day, and any other days with food involved in the celebration."

"You're only here to eat my cookin'? It has nothing to do with finding your Mate?"

"You know I would walk a hundred miles, barefooted in the snow, to eat your food. You are one helluva cook."

"Why thank you, Caspian, my boy."

"And to answer your second question, no," he adamantly denied, meaning it with all his heart. "Why would I come here to find her? I know Bane said it was a matter of some urgency that I find her, but he also said that my Mate would be with Sydney Kavanaugh. Now, since I have no idea where in all of God with a capital G's great green Earth she is, nor do I want to take my happy heinie how ever many miles under the sand into some frozen cave to find out if Bane's had another vision or prophecy or whatever the hell it is he has when he sees the future, I came to see you, one of my favorite people in all the world."

"Hey!" A deep, rumbling voice floated from the backdoor a second before the thud of boots on the hardwood floor followed. "Is that the one and only Caspian MacAllen trying to sweet talk *my* Auntie Barbara?"

Getting to his feet, Cass smiled wide and put out his hand as Jed slid his in for a shake. As they shook, the Guardsman felt the connection of not only their heritage but their combined history, respect, and brotherly love.

Being older than all the MacAllen boys, Cass and Jed spent many good times exploring the MacAllen Ranch with Owen and Barbara before Gage came along. Then they became the Three Musketeers, and the real fun began.

Cass and Jed even experienced their first Shifts within hours of one another, under the full moon, in McKitterick Canyon, halfway between the back fence of the Ranch and the Magical entrance to the Reservation. Being much younger, Gage had missed the fun, but they'd been sure to prepare him for what was to come.

Together, the three boys were unstoppable, and although Cass hadn't seen Jed in years, not much had changed. One look into the dark brown, almost black eyes of the Stallion Shifter, and the memories came rushing back.

Walking under the bright, white light of the Yuletide Full Moon, the frozen sand abraded his bare feet as the winter winds whipped in every direction, beating at the flesh of his chest. It was the seventh night in a row that he'd paced the same path, and it was the first few hours of Christmas Eve. Unable to sleep, unwilling to stay inside, he'd prayed for the December weather to wash away whatever was haunting him and allow him to once again slumber as only a teenage boy can.

Visions of the land he loved, nocturnal animals of every kind running to and fro, the lush array of foliage, and the multitude of crops of the MacAllen Ranch contrasting with the taupe, brown, and red clay of the Chihuahuan Desert filled every corner of his mind—but the view was askew. It was so different than what he knew so well. Instead of seeing it from his already six-foot stature, the fourteen-year-old was looking down from a great height, taking in all he'd ever surveyed in a single glance.

The Magic of the Ancients thrummed with a vigor he'd never before felt, and the Enchantment of the Great Creator spoke to him in ways he'd only ever heard of in the stories his mom, dad, aunt, uncles, and grandpa told. Something had awakened within him, something he'd known was coming but, for some reason, was resisting. There was a tug of war going on in his soul, but both sides were simply holding steady.

Cass thought about talking to Owen. He'd even gone out to the barn just that morning to talk to the Leader of the MacAllen Dragons. But when he opened his mouth to speak, the words refused to be spoken. Over and over, he tried, and over and over, nothing happened.

He could talk about the saddle Owen was repairing and the beautiful Mustang Mare he'd finally gotten to take a carrot out of his hand. Hell, he was even able to recount the conversation he'd had with Jed Thorntree about the Texas Baseball League finally getting a footing in Houston. But no matter how hard he tried, Cass simply could not bring himself to talk about all the weird thoughts and feelings wreaking havoc in his mind.

As a last-ditch effort, he'd gone to the Res to Chief Cheveyo and his sons, Dasan and Elan. Since his mom was one of the Tribe, and her Mating with his dad had been blessed by the Great Creator and all the Chiefs, that meant Cass was also a Thorntree Cherokee. Having such an extensive extended family had been such a comfort after losing his parents at such a young age. He'd shared everything with them. So, why was he suddenly finding it hard to talk to them about what really mattered?

No, he wasn't the only person, or child, to lose those he held most dear to the Skeenah Legion. Jed's parents had also gone to the Heavens during the bloodiest battle of the war. Cass believed it was one of the many things that bound them as brothers tighter than blood ever could.

During the Clash at Guadalupe Peak, the one that finally brought peace to their land, everyone who could fight did, and his parents were no different. Not only were they defending their people and their land, but they were also fighting for their freedom, their way of life, and their belief in the Universe and the Great Creator.

Too young to join the fight, Cass had been taken to stay with Barbara, who was pregnant with her second son. He would never forget looking into his father's eyes as he heard his low rumble reassuring, "Caspian Thomas MacAllen, you are the Hope. You are the best of all of us. Know that you are loved, my son. Never forget that you are loved."

Looking at his momma, he tried hard not to cry, but the tears fell when she whispered, "Oh, my little Agiyvsdi, what an amazing young man you have grown to be, and what a great man you will be. Every day and in every way, you make me proud to be your momma. Remember your Faith in the Ancients of All, the Great Creator, and the Universe. As your daddy said, you are the Hope. Know that you are loved and that one day, that Love will come in the form of your Mate. She will see who you really are and love you all the more for it." Kissing him on the forehead, she pulled back and added, "Your daddy and I will always be with you."

It wasn't until much later that Cass realized his parents knew they wouldn't be coming home. For a long time, he was angry. He resented them. He was pissed off at the people who'd come home.

Well, except Owen. For some reason, that rage was never pointed at his uncle, but it was alive and well with regard to others. He could feel blinding hatred trying to take root in his soul every time he saw a mom or a dad with their child.

On one of the worst days, the wee hours of the morning of Christmas Eve, he'd gone to Guadalupe Peak, the highest point in the entire state of Texas. The trek had been hard and long. Cass had fallen more than once and thought about giving up with almost every step he'd taken, but his need to see where his parents gave their lives was stronger than all the other feelings.

Once there, he'd been greeted by a very large, obviously very lazy Black Bear. Laying there, only its eyes moving, the Yonah—Bear in the Cherokee language—did nothing more than grunt in Cass's direction.

Halfway through his journey to the battlefield, the young man turned to find the Bear had gotten up and followed. Instantly enraged that the time he needed with the ghosts of his parents was being interrupted, Cass growled, "Go away. I want to be alone."

No sooner had he spoken the words than the Black Bear transformed into a six-foot woman with long red curls and the stature of an Amazon. Wearing a deep, rich brown, tanned deer-skin vest, leggings, and breechcloth, she was an imposing figure he instantly knew was used to being respected, if not revered.

Taking in the large, colorfully beaded chest plate adorned with hand-forged silver medallions, Cass was immediately aware that he was in the presence of greatness. Then his gaze landed on the spear carved from the holy Cedar tree with a head shaped from white granite, and there was absolutely no doubt he was in the presence of a true Cherokee Warrior, the Leader of the Ditlihi, the Chief of the Chosen Warriors.

Before he could speak, she reached into the thick fall of auburn hair lying on her shoulder, pulled out the wing feather of the Sacred Bird, a Bald Eagle, and held it in the space between them. *Unsure what to do, but knowing if he didn't take the gift, he would be insulting the Great Creator's Chosen Warrior, the young man held out his hands.*

Having been taught the ways of the Cherokee Nation by some of the most honorable Ani-Yunwiya, Real People to those of the Tribe, Cass accepted the token, bowed his head, and reverently acknowledged, "Thank you, Noble Ditlihi, for this gift. I shall wear it with pride and remember the day I was in the presence of the Great Creator's Chosen Warrior."

Gasping when just the tips of her fingers softly touched the underside of his chin, Cass allowed her to lift his face until he looked deep into her dark brown eyes. Watching gold flecks swirl as a Magic that could be none other than Mother Nature's wrapped over and around them with the unconditional love and acceptance that can only come from an adoring Omnipotent Being.

"Can you feel that, Uktena?" *Not waiting for an answer, she continued,* "You are loved. Like the Eagle from which that feather fell, you are strong. You have great courage. You embrace your freedom and want the same for all others. You were blessed by the Sacred Bird at the moment of your birth."

Without another word, she let her hand drop and took a step back. Raising the spear she held at her side, she pointed toward the Reservation. "Those are your people." *Then she turned and pointed to the MacAllen Ranch.* "Those are also your people."

Returning to face him, she stood perfectly still for what seemed like forever but was truly only a second. When she spoke again, Cass could feel the magnitude of her words. "In your heart, all are your people. In the days to come, you will be asked to make a choice. It will not be concerning who you love, who you protect, or who you call Family. Neither the Great Creator nor the

Universe would ever be so callous. They know your heart and have seen you are more than worthy."

Smiling, the expression brightening not only her face but all of Guadalupe Peak, she continued. "The decision you will be asked to make—the choice—will be simple. No sooner will the question be asked than your heart and soul give you the answer. Trust your heart. Listen to your soul. Believe in all you've been taught. Know that you are loved, Caspian Thomas MacAllen. Believe that you are the Hope."

Before his brain had time to catch up with his mouth, Cass blurted out, "That's what my mom and dad said. It was the last thing they said to me. How could you have known?" Shaking his head and then running his fingers through the messy curls atop his head, he didn't wait for an answer but hurried to add, "It doesn't matter how you knew. I came here tonight to... to... to..."

Once again, closing the distance between them, the Ditlihi laid her hand on his shoulder. "You came here for answers, and I came here to give them to you."

Taking her hand off his shoulder, she motioned toward the battlefield where his parents lost their Earthly lives and ascended into the Heavens. "Your mother and father were great warriors. Esta Evilhawk and Thomas MacAllen, their names will forever be written on my heart. I was there that night. I had the honor of not only calling them Sidanelv, my Family, but seeing how very much they loved you."

"But they... they....:

"No, Caspian, you are wrong," she corrected when he couldn't say the words. "They did not choose to leave you; they chose to give you life. They made the ultimate sacrifice, not of their own lives, but of a long life with you to preserve the Light and extinguish the Darkness. They willingly, bravely, and with all the faith I have ever seen in my long life ran toward the enemy, toward The Skeenah Legion, when they realized that I, along *with the Nûñnë'hï, could not save every Warrior of the Light. They fought more courageously than any other I have ever witnessed, and they look down from the Heavens every minute of every day with love and pride at the man you are becoming."*

He didn't have the words. His mind had sufficiently been blown. This woman, the Warrior, the Being, who was chosen by the Great Creator to protect all Ani-Yunwiya, had come to this place on this night to speak to him about his parents. She was there to..."

"I am here to prepare you for the decision you must make and ensure that your heart is without doubt, fear, or hate, and you do not blame your parents for the choices they made. I have been sent by the Great Creator and the Universe to be sure you see the Truth."

Slowly nodding just once, she speared him a look that he felt in every fiber of his being. Time stood still. Cass didn't move. He didn't blink. Hell, he didn't even breathe.

Finally, when he was sure he would pass out, the young MacAllen exhaled as the Ditlihi added, "You are loved, Caspian MacAllen. You are the Hope. Watch for the signs. Follow your heart and soul when faced with decisions. And always look for the Nûñnë'hï. One of those very special People Who Will Live Forever is the key to your happiness, to your happily ever after."

Before he could take another breath or say a word, the Warrior was gone. Not even the Black Bear remained. Cass was alone, and for the first time since he'd lost his parents, it didn't bother him at all.

Walking to the center of the battlefield, he saw the outline of the crater that had opened up and swallowed The Skeenah Legion. As far as the eye could see, the echo of the souls of the righteous who had fought to protect the world cast long shadows. They didn't move. They didn't moan. They were nothing like the comic books or stories would have people believe.

No, they were stoic. They stood tall. They stood guard. They were the Favored. They had been called to defend the Light and had run headlong into the Darkness with no thought of their own wellbeing.

Slowly traversing the entire area, he prayed to see the shadowy figures of his parents. His heart and soul willed it to happen, but it was not meant to be.

As the winds became stronger, some of the gusts nearly knocked him backward. The temperature dropped, and the mercury flirted with that elusive zero mark.

Heading back to the trail, he slowly and carefully inched his way down. Ascending had been much easier than descending. Gravity was a strange and unforgiving Mistress.

The sharp, narrow turns, no wider than two feet, were nearly impossible. With the wind pushing and swirling in every direction, his fingers and hands were raw from grabbing the jagged, sharp limestone and sedimentary rock that formed the massive formation.

When the balls of his feet finally touched down on the ice-covered sands of the Chihuahuan Desert, the pounding of running footfalls cut through the blustery breeze. Turning one way and then the other, he finally caught sight of Jed Thorntree racing toward him, his long, dark hair flowing behind him like the mane of a great Stallion.

The moment the boys were within shouting distance, a flash of bright white light followed by a blazing bolt of Ancient Magic shot from the Heavens. Eyes locked on the glowing sphere rising from the sand, Cass could not believe what he saw.

Then a deep baritone with a thick Scottish brogue that reminded him of Grandpa MacAllen spoke from somewhere deep within him, asking, "Tell me, Caspian Thomas MacAllen, do you choose Uktena or will your Fate and your Destiny belong to the Wa ya?"

3

"**W**hat do you mean you met *my* Mate?" Abbie didn't mean to sound so demanding. The only excuse she had was that it felt as if her heart was about to beat out of her chest, and as usual, her mouth took over long before her brain got into the swing of things. No matter how hard she tried, the words just kept coming. "How did you meet him? How do you know it was him? I thought..."

"You thought right," Sydney blessedly interrupted. I *did* go home for the birth of my sister and to tell Mom and Dad I was back, but I didn't get to see them or even stay for very long because..."

"Oh, yeah." Tapping the center of her forehead with the tips of her fingers, Abbie huffed, "I am *so* sorry. You were in the middle of telling me about hearing Garrett's voice, and my mind decided to take a little hike to the distant past, and then my mouth went into overdrive. I am *so* sorry. Please tell me what he said and what I can do to help. I didn't mean to be so needy."

"You are never ever *never* needy," Syd reassured, letting a sense of calm and true affection flow. "I understand. Believe me, I understand. That's why I need to tell you what I know. So..." She winked. "Like I said..."

Once again, Abbie couldn't stay quiet. She felt as if she was looking over a cliff, trying to decide whether to jump and fly or turn around and run like Hell.

"Like you said, something earth-shattering is about to happen in my life." Shaking her head, she held up her hands and pushed at the space between them when her friend tried to interrupt. "But you're right here, right now, and you heard the voice of *your* Mate. So, whatever is comin' my way will have to wait. I just gotta ask, and not because I am not as happy as a pig in mud to see ya', why are you *here* and not over there with the Blue Thunder Clan waking that boy up with kisses? He. Spoke. To. You. You need to get while the gettin's good. Come on, Girlie. You know what I mean." Waggling her eyebrows, she added a shoulder shake and a click of her tongue. "You get to be Princess Charming, waking up your Prince from his deep sleep with a sweet kiss that turns into a hot one, and the *bow-chica-wowow* follows."

"Goddess be, I do so love you."

"And I love you, so out with it."

"Well," Syd sighed, all the fun falling out of her like someone had untied the string, and all the air had rushed out. Then, blowing out an incredibly long-suffering breath, she matter-of-factly stated, "I'm here and not there because he isn't there."

"Wait! What? Garrett woke up and left the Blue Thunder Lair without telling you. He didn't call to you? Nobody called you?"

"Oh, they called me, alright, but it was a few hours after the fact, and partly because the *Rianadair*–the Trackers," she explained the Gaelic. "...they sent out to locate him could not find the first clue. Like nothing–not a damn thing–which is the strangest thing because he was barefooted."

She stopped and inhaled so deeply that her shoulders raised close to the glittering stones in the lobes of her ears. As she exhaled, she continued, "Apparently, all traces of Garrett, even his scent, disappeared about a foot from the small back gate that not everybody knows is there. It was weird. They aren't used to not finding something, to having answers of some kind. They didn't want to worry me unnecessarily. Unfortunately, it was seriously necessary when all was said and done, and I wish they hadn't waited, but I can't second guess decisions made by others in the past. Then, after talking with Della, Niall, Calysta, and Maddox..."

"Oh no! You had to talk to the grumpy, old Mad Dragon? How is he? How is his gorgeous and perfectly Witchy Mate, Calysta? I haven't seen them in at least a month of Sundays. They both helped me understand a little more about my inherited Magic."

"Oh, yeah, I remember you tellin' me about that," Syd nodded. "They're both really good," she snickered. "Maddox is still grumpy but with a lot more soft edges than he ever had. Calysta is wonderful, as usual, and really good for the old coot. They are really good for each other.

"I bet." Abbie chuckled, then gasped. "Sorry again," she quickly apologized. "I promise to keep my lips zipped until you're done tellin' me what's goin' on with that Dragon of yours." Pretending to zip her lips, lock the imaginary lock on the opposite side, and throw away the key, she motioned for her bestie to continue.

"You are the best. I just love you so much. Shavon was right. We were always meant to me friends. Just being in your orbit makes me feel better, and it's not just your heritage, your Nûññë'hï blood and Magic making me feel better. It's you, my friend. Never forget that it's you. You give people, no, wait, you give *me* Hope." Giving Abbie a quick hug, she hurried on. "Okay, no more procrastinating. I've already fed your ego enough," she winked and chuckled. "Okay, where was I? Oh, yeah. Before I got the call, I was doing my normal thing. I was on the way to the Blue Thunder Clan to see Garrett before heading to see Mom and Dad. I wanted to surprise them. I knew, no, check, I *thought* I knew that I had a couple more weeks before the baby was due, but our Baby Orla just couldn't wait." Smiling, she winked and went on. "Why we expected her to wait is a mystery to me. She's got Mom and Dad's blood in her veins. She will wait for nothing–*ever*. We definitely have that in common." Pausing, she smiled, and that time, it reached her eyes.

"I was about halfway there when Della called." With a knowing look, she tapped her temple with the tip of her index finger. "Her panic was palpable. It was like a tsunami roaring into my brain like waves in the Other Realm just outside the Citadel gates." Waving the thought away, she focused, "She was talking so fast it was hard to keep up. I got the part about things being crazy over there right off the bat. Some kind of weird virus worked its way through the kids who aren't one hundred percent Dragon or Supernatural. Thank the Great Goddess and God with a capital G. They were able to get it contained and everyone is better. I'm pretty sure she just said all that to work up the nerve for what was coming. I was just about to congratulate her when, without so much as a breath, she just blurted out, *'Garrett's gone.' We didn't even know he was awake. It had only been a few hours. Maybe less since I last checked on him. You know I never leave him alone for long when you're not here. I never want him– or anyone for that matter–to feel abandoned in our Clinic.*

Anyway, I went in to be sure he was okay, have a little one-way chat, and check all his labs and He. Was. Gone."

"Of course, I freaked out and started talking almost as fast as she was." Sydney stopped, took a deep breath, and pushed the curls off her shoulders, a nervous tick Abbie had witnessed from her bestie at least a hundred times. "That was when she told me about the *Rianadair*. I mean, they sent the best of the best. The guys that teach all the others. Force Rianadair is led by the old guy, Daire, and he's got Fergus, Haim, and Wynn trained to be almost as good as he is. You know them, don't you?"

Nodding because she wasn't about to interrupt Sydney's flow, Abbie smiled. She knew it wasn't the time to remind her bestie that they had met the Rianadair when they were together on the Isle of Skye almost five years ago.

With a rather vehement swoosh of her hand, Abbie opened her eyes wide and spoke directly into her friend's mind, *"Get back to the story, Lady. Don't make me get all 'just the facts, ma'am' on you like Declan."*

"Ha! That's a good one," Sydney acknowledged aloud, then got right back to what she was saying. "Sorry, you know how I get when I'm nervous. But I promise to stay focused."

Straightening her spine and rolling back her shoulders, she continued. "So, the only thing we could think was that Garrett really had been able to hear me as I sat there for hours just droning on and on about anything and everything." She snickered. "I literally ran out of things to say about six months ago and told him about this bracelet I'd watched Emma, Andrew O'Brien's Mate and one heck of a jewelry artist, making. I don't think you've met her yet, but you will. Anywho, all talk of anything but Mom and Dad having a baby and how excited I am to be a big sister is pretty much all he'd heard for the last couple of months. To me, it made sense that he would think I was with them at the Golden Fire Lair."

Holding up her index finger, Abbie waited until Syd nodded before she blurted out, "How many freakin' people know that you're back? It just dawned on me that every time you talked about being with Garrett, Della and the others had to have seen you. How in the hell have they kept your secret? Even better, how in all that's holy has everybody kept it from your mom and dad? Let's be honest, good news usually spreads like Dragon Fire at the Annual Beltane Festival, and you bein' home has to be the best news ever."

"Well, that is all Shavon's doing. When I'm there..." She opened her hands and pointed left and right at the same time. "Ya' know, home or with Carrick's Clan or even up in the Arctic with Lore and Sable–places where people recognize me–we talk and have fun. Everything's pretty normal. However, the minute I leave, they pretty much don't remember me." She stopped, looked up for a split second, then added, "Well, not pretty much. They just don't remember I was there at all."

"But..."

"But you still do? That's what you were gonna say, right?"

"Umm, yeah."

Syd nodded. "And so does Kyndel, Rayne, and a few others. That's because I asked Shavon to make a little change to the Magical Charm thingy she and I put together. I just needed to have some interaction with people in *this* Realm. I mean, I had to go to the Refuge and the Citadel. Plain and simple, it was just what had to happen. But I always knew I would come back home. I would be living here–in the Realm–most of the time. Therefore, I needed the practice. I had gotten way too used to speaking telepathically, moving things with little more than a thought, and doing things like most of the residents of the Citadel do."

"Well, shit, I didn't think of that. Ten years living one way and growing up at many times the normal rate definitely trumps the first six years of your 'human' life as far as everyday life goes."

"It all took me a while to get used, to understand, too," Sydney reassured. "I didn't think about all the minutiae at the time for a long time. I got used to how things were there, but I never forgot home and where I wanted to be. When Shavon said it was time to start reintegrating myself, I was just so excited to come back and visit. I agreed to everything she said. After the first few times, it was so damned hard. I spent most of my time explaining the same things I'd explained the first time. I just had to have her change it. It was *so* hard. I kept thinking I might mess up and forget something. Hell, I said it so many times that I wasn't even sure what was coming out of my mouth."

"Oh, my stars and garters, I never even thought of that," Abbie inhaled. "Guess you had it all figured out when we met."

"Yeah, pretty much."

"Okay, enough of that. Please, get back to what happened next with ya' boy. You got as far as you went to the Golden Fire Clan because it was the only place you could think that Garrett would go. Is that right?"

"Exactly right, but he wasn't there. As a matter of fact, I only got as far as telling everybody in the room I had come there lookin' for him when Dad roared into everybody's brains that the baby was on the way. Rayne, Kyndel, well, hell, everybody in the house, even Jay and the newest set of O'Brien twins, ran out the door faster than I've ever seen them move."

Getting a faraway look in her eyes, Sydney's gaze went back to McKittrick Creek. Sitting still, trying to be patient, Abbie could feel the doubt and fear returning to brew inside her friend. It quite literally took everything in her not to demand that Syd talk, to put *her* out of her misery, but she persevered. Then the blond bit the inside of her cheek, and she had to do something.

Touching Syd's shoulder, she waited until those pretty blue peepers were looking her way before gently nudging, "You were running across the Lair with everyone else, and that was when..."

Slowly nodding as she spoke, Syd picked up where she'd left off. The words came slowly at first. Thank the Heavens, it didn't take long until she was on a roll. "...when Garrett whispered, '*Where are you, Mo charaid? I can't find you.*' directly into my mind. It was seriously the weirdest, most wonderful thing I'd ever felt in my whole life. I knew who it was, but I'd never heard his voice before, so it almost scared the living crap right out of me. He was also speaking the oldest of the Ancient Dragon Language, so it took my mind a second to translate."

"But none of that mattered. I stopped so fast that my feet skidded. I for sure thought my butt was gonna hit the soggy, muddy ground. Luckily, I stayed upright, and my jeans stayed clean. I just waited. I couldn't think. I couldn't breathe. Hell, I couldn't do anything but wait for what I knew, what I could *feel* was coming next."

"Looking around, head snaping left and right, everybody raced past me like I wasn't there. Then I realized that for them, I wasn't there. Somehow, someway, when I heard Garrett's voice, I triggered Shavon's Magic, and bibbidy-bobbedy-boo, I was invisible."

"Holy shit! You gotta show me that trick. It would be so

cool to be able to just *poof* away with little more than a thought."

"I don't think I could do it again even if some idiot had a gun loaded with silver bullets pointed at my head." Her chuckle was forced. "It's all Shavon. I'm not sure how it works. I haven't gotten that far in my teachings, and I'm thinkin' it's way farther down the road."

Reaching for her friend's hands before she realized she'd moved, Abbie poured love and understanding into their connection. Seeing some of the beautiful rosy color return to Syd's cheeks, she coaxed, and only because she knew her friend needed to talk, "Did he say anything else?"

"He did, but it took a minute, and when he finally spoke, it was a freakin' whispered riddle."

"A riddle? What the hell?"

"I thought stronger words than that," Syd snorted almost happily. "Why would he wake up, go on a walkabout, then call out to me with a damn riddle? I mean, it dadgum sure sounded like a riddle to me. He said, '*Mo ghràdh, Mo Anam Aharaid...*'" She stopped and winked, "I have to admit, just to you, that my heart did a silly little pitter-pat when he called me his love and his Soul Mate."

"As well it should have," Abbie wholeheartedly agreed. "That boy needs to say all kinds of nice things to you, kiss you silly, sweep you off your feet, and then live happily ever after right by your side for the rest of forever and then some. I know I can't wait to hear those words from the man-made for me by the Universe." She dropped her chin and narrowed her eyes. "And you're the only one I'mma gonna admit that to. So, if you tell anyone else, I'll swear you're lyin'."

Drawing a cross over her heart with her free hand, Syd

raised it in a Girl Scout salute and solemnly promised, "I swear, I will never tell." Then she laughed long and loud.

When they could both breathe again, Abbie chuckled, "Okay, keep goin'. I just gotta know the riddle part. Maybe we can work it out together."

"You got it," Syd nodded. "He said, *'I do not know where I am, Mo stór. I thought I knew, but everything has changed. With the sand overhead and the ice underfoot, I can find you nowhere.'*"

Letting go of Syd's hand, Abbie giggled, "Okay, yep, that's a riddle." It didn't matter that she sounded like a schoolgirl. It made her friend grin, and that made it so worthwhile.

"That's what I thought too, and I answered with, 'I know where you are. I'm on my way.' But he said, "*No, Mo ghràdh, do not come to me. Go to the Nûññë'hï, the sister of your heart. Lead her to the Dragon made for her by the Universe. You know who he is, and he is nearby your friend. An old enemy threatens our kin and hers. Go, Sydney, Mo chridhe. Go to where the sands meet the sky, where the Timber Wolf, the Dragon, and the Big Cats stand side by side, guarding the ones who need them. We will find one another when the time is right'.*"

Silence filled the meadow as the women stared at one another. Abbie had no clue what to say, and it was obvious Sydney felt the same way. Had it not been for a couple of trout jumping around in the water, making more noise than usual, they might have stayed that way for hours.

"Wow," was all Abbie could say. "That is... That is..."

"That is some serious shit," Syd jested. "And this has to be where he wanted me to come. I mean, you're the only Nûññë'hï I know."

"Good thing, since I'm the only one around right now. Well, the only one alive."

"See? I do listen."

"I know you do, Goofball."

"Even though I knew where he wanted me to go, I still stood there–invisible and in the middle of the pasture at the back of the Golden Fire Lair with people running past me– for a few minutes. Okay, longer than a few minutes. It took me *a good little while* to figure out what I should do. I finally gave in and called Shavon. She said I needed to listen to Garrett. She, and the other Oracles, are of the belief that the Black Magic bullshit is gone from Garrett's system. She said that everything Calysta, Niall, and Della have done–all the Healing Rituals, the Spells, the herbal remedies, even calling Bane and a few other Dragons who are doctors to do whatever they do that no one else can–healed what needed to be healed and got rid of all the negative shit. They, I mean the Oracles and Seers, believe that for the last year or two, he's been in some kind of contact with the Ancients."

"The Ancient Dragon Elders?"

"Well, see, that's where I can't get a straight answer."

"Which means?"

"Well, I assumed it was the Dragons. He is a Dragon Guardsman, but Shavon kept telling me not to take anything for granted. When I asked, like I said, I never got a straight answer, ya' know?"

"On yeah, I know. I've met that tall, gorgeous drink of water. I know just as sure as God with a G made little green apples that she told you not to assume because it makes an ass outta you and me," Abbie laughed out loud.

Laughing along, Sydney teased, "She didn't say those exact words, but it was damn sure implied."

"I do so love that girl, if for no reason because she brought us together."

"Yes, ma'am, me too." Raising her hand, Syd teased, "You better not leave me hangin'. I know it's not cool, but I need a high five."

Slapping her friend's hand, Abbie chuckled, "We really are the biggest nerds."

"Yep, it makes us the best."

"Damn straight." Sitting in comfortable, companionable silence, they both watched the trout swimming in the cool, crisp water for what seemed like an hour when Abbie jumped to her feet and said, "Come on back to the Res with me. I've got a freezer full of leftovers, some of Barbara MacAllen's special blend of coffee with all those good spices, and a tin of her cookies and cupcakes. We can put on our jammies, eat on the couch, and watch corny rom coms while we figure out what to do next."

Standing up almost as fast as she had, Syd clapped her hands and did a little happy dance. "That's sounds awesome. Lead the way."

Walking down the creek bank, the ladies had just reached the footbridge Abbie kept painted with different flowers for every season when Sydney stopped, laid her hand on Abbie's arm, and whispered, "There was something I forgot to tell you."

Instantly worried, she spun on her toes and practically demanded, "What? What did you forget? Are you okay? Do we need to go see a doctor? Bane is out there in that frozen cave in the desert. I can have you there in the blink of an eye. Or we can..."

"You can chill out," Syd snickered. "It's nothing like that."

"Then what is it?"

"We both got so wrapped up in my story that we forgot all about your Mate? The guy I met? The one..."

"Oh shit!" Abbie laughed out loud. "I did. I forgot all about what you said." Slapping at the air as if she was swatting away a gnat, she went on, "Pfft, you can tell me when we get to the house. If he's all the way over there, then...."

"But he's not all the way over there," Syd countered. "Not if what Garrett said is right or if I heard his last name right when Kyndel introduced us."

"No. No way. You can't mean the..." Shaking her head with such fury that her long red curls went back and forth in front of her face, Abbie added, "I know all of Barbara and Owen's boys. All but one is Mated, and Colton is like a brother. I would've known if we were..."

"There's no other MacAllen Dragons galloping around this big blue and green marble?"

"Well..." Abbie stopped, turned, put her hands on the wooden rail of the footbridge, and tried to recall everything she knew of the MacAllen Family. It was easier to say it out loud, so she started at the beginning. "Well, as you know, Barbara and my mom were friends growing up, along with another girl, Esta. The three of them were darn near inseparable if the stories I was told were right. When Barb brought Owen to meet the Chief, he and my dad became instant buddies. Then, not long after, Esta's Mate ended up being one of Owen's brothers who had come for the Mating Ceremony. From what I know, the three couples were really tight, even after Esta and Thomas had a son. Of course, it was only about five or maybe six years later when Barb and Owen had Gage."

Thinking a little harder, it took a few minutes, but she soon added, "I was really little and mostly stayed on the Res, but I remember Jed bringing a boy about his age home all the time. They were best buds, always up to something, but rarely anything bad. I think he might have been a MacAllen." Turning back to Syd, she rolled her eyes and shook her head, "But I was in the same room or playground or maybe even the same tree with that boy more than once. I would've..."

"You were a little girl, right?"

"Well, yeah."

"And he was a little boy?"

"Older than me, but yeah, we were both really young."

"He wasn't close to his first Shift, and you were nowhere near twenty-one, right?"

"You know we weren't."

"Then it is completely possible that you have also already met your Mate, and you were both too young for the Mating Magic to do its thing."

"That just can't..."

"Oh, yes, it can be true." Sydney was adamant. "Take it from the girl who's spent a lot of the last ten years of her life not only getting older at a rate that defies pretty much everything we ever knew but also learning the history of the Dragons, the Thorntree Timber Wolves, the Oracles, and even more than a little bit about the Nûññë'hi. Anything, and I say this with all earnest, *any-eeee-thing*, is possible in the world in which we live."

"Well, shit and Shinola," Abbie groaned. "Guess we better go see a Cherokee Chief about a Dragon, huh?

4

I t took less than a second for Cass to do what he knew was right. His heart and soul called out to him, telling him what he must do. But he knew the right decision. Had always known the only decision he would make. His Destiny was as clear as the nose on his face. There had never been a doubt, and he did exactly what had to be done.

"I, Caspian Thomas MacAllen, am Uktena. I am Dragon."

"Very well, young Uktena. So you have answered. So it shall be. You are Dragon."

The very second the decree had been spoken, time sped up to an unimaginable, blurring rate. The scenery whirled around him with such velocity that Guadalupe Mountain went from his right to his left in the blink of an eye. The frozen sand, tiny prisms in their crystalline form, levitated, spinning in one direction, each on their own axis as they rotated around him the opposite way.

The blustery wind whipped as it had been, but in that moment, it spoke to him. The howl turned to a roar, and the words became clear, unmistakable, and reaffirming. *"Today, Caspian Thomas MacAllen, you are who you were always meant to be. Within you lies the heart of the Dragon King, Blár. As of today, you are one. This heritage is a gift from your father. It was ordained and blessed by the Universe, the Great Goddess, and all The Powers That Be. Together, you will do great things. In whatever form you choose to take—you are a Guardsman. As the Chosen Universe's Warriors, you will defend Dragonkin, humankind, and all the Earth and its many inhabitants against Evil in all its forms. And you will not be alone."*

Had the voice gone? Was that all it had to say? Was he supposed to figure out the rest for himself? Many times, his dad said there was no manual for being a Guardsman.

The silence was deafening. Even the wind ceased to blow, the sand hung in the air, and the ground stilled under his feet. His heart skipped a beat.

Then everything began again. The voice boomed. Its resonance was more profound, more gripping. *"You are not only two. You are also three. For although you have chosen the Dragon—you are Dragon—and will possess the monumental ability to Transform into all his many forms, the Timber Wolf Alpha, Faolan, will also reside within your soul. Like his ancestors before him, King Faolan carries with him the Magic of the Moon. He possesses tremendous intuition and transformative abilities—not of the Shift, but of the mind and soul—and he will forever be the Ruler of the Hunt and the Speaker for the Dead, all of which he will share with you. This is the gift from your mother, Esta Evilhawk, a proud Cherokee, Spiritual Elder, and even prouder parent. Never forget, Caspian Thomas MacAllen, you are the Hope."*

"Furthermore, when you find your Mate and your union is blessed by the Universe, and you wear the Mating Mark, you and she will become The Everlasting Hope. Do not take this lightly. Do not ignore the signs. You must know that Hope is the companion of Power. It is the catalyst for success in whatever

form it may take. Those who believe in Hope, who harness that unstoppable Power with all the strength they have within their heart and soul, will receive the gift of miracles. Together, you and your Mate will be the only defense this Earth, and all its inhabitants have against the Scourge on Thundering Hooves that shall try to infest and invade all living creatures. And that, dear Dragon, is Everlasting Hope.

"Go forth, Caspian Thomas MacAllen. Live the life befitting of your Blessing. Be open to everything. Use all you've been given for the Good and the Light. When the day comes, the woman made for you by the Universe will find you, and together, you will accomplish great things."

Trying to formulate the words, the questions whizzing through his mind so quickly he couldn't separate one from another, Cass stopped short when the smoldering chasm created by the original bolt of incredibly old Mysticism opened wider. Expanding and growing, the ground once again shook beneath his feet as the light grew brighter, warmer, and more present than even Jed standing just a few feet from him.

Moving of their own volition, his feet took one step and then another until he was marching with untold confidence toward the glowing, growing, surging mass of the most powerful Magic he'd ever felt. Stopping at the edge, his toes floating on nothing but highly charged atmosphere, Cass was ready to take the final step. He was prepared to do whatever had to be done. He would fall into the bottomless crater, knowing that no harm would befall him. He had answered the call of the Ancients as the Ditlihi told him to, and he would continue to abide by her instruction, come what may.

He was following his heart and soul–and the Dragon King with whom he shared his soul. The Magic, the Mysticism, the utterly pure Enchantment of the Earth, of Mother Nature, of Chaos, of all The Powers That Be were calling to him. They were telling him that everything he needed at that moment was in the core of the Flames ignited at the birth of Everything.

Eyes raising to the Heavens, he took the last step. Waiting to fall. Knowing it was what he had to do. Another miracle happened. Instead of plummeting into an unfathomable fiery abyss, Cass slowly floated upward.

Higher and higher, riding the Flames, the golden light that he somehow knew had always been there, the one he knew belonged to the Dragon King with whom he shared his soul, burst to life. The sheer magnitude of its strength and influence, its utter command of *everything*, was staggering, and before Cass had time to truly appreciate the experience, he was on fire from the inside out.

Back bowing until he literally formed the shape of an upside-down letter U, his mouth opened so wide that his jaws cracked, and the sound that flew from his lips was one of pure anguish. Head snapping forward, his lanky frame was instantly bent in half the other way. His arms flew out to the side with such intensity the balls of his shoulder joints were torn from their sockets before instantly being knit back together stronger than ever before.

Levitating high above the Flames, his body was stretched to its fullest height. The cracking of bone and the tearing of joints and muscles filled his mind as the flesh covering his spine sizzled and bubbled.

The pain, the anguish, the utter agony stole the breath from his lungs. In and out of consciousness, the ringing in his ears grew louder with each passing second as black dots danced before his eyes.

He was going to pass out. Unconsciousness was hovering

just out of reach, and he prayed for it to come. If only he could rest for just a moment and receive the tiniest bit of respite. He knew if he could, he would have the strength to finish. Sadly, as it was, the young Dragon was in so much pain that he was going to miss the glory of his first Shift.

It was demoralizing. It was damn near debilitating. It was unfathomable, and he simply refused to let the unthinkable happen. He was strong. He was blessed. He was Caspian Thomas MacAllen, dammit, and he shared his soul with the legendary Dragon King, Blár.

Reaching for the Magic he'd inherited from his parents, the fortitude of the MacAllen Dragons, and the magnitude of the Thorntree Timber Wolves, his soul, his *Hope* touched the Heavens. Literally wrapping his hands around the brilliantly glowing strands of the oldest Enchantment the world had ever known, Cass was instantly and completely in control. He *was* the Master of his Destiny. No longer was he a victim of the Shift. He–along with his Dragon King–now directed the Miracle of Transformation as it had always been intended.

Gone was the pain. Washed away was all frailty. His body was restored. His bones were longer and stronger. His muscles had grown larger, more powerful. He was on the precipice of greatness, and Cass was ready to accept all that he was to be.

Landing next to Jed with an earthshaking thud, the balls of his feet triggered the True Shift, the one he would always embrace–the Conversion of the Dragon King who would become a Legendary Guardsman. Spreading his arms wide, the tips of the fingers of his left hand brushed Jed's shoulder. A spark of recognition, a jolt of electricity that he was sure could've lit up the whole state of Texas for several years, shot through both of them, and Cass knew that as he

Shifted into the great Dragon King Blár, Jed would Transform into the Black Stallion with whom he shared his soul.

Eyes meeting, the boys acknowledged they were about
to become men in the way of Shifterkin, and each focused
on what had to be done. Cass's gaze flew to his arms. He
smiled as the crystalline blue scales flashed to life just under
the skin. Pushing through the flesh, they were brilliantly
incandescent and more striking than he ever could have
imagined.

Once again, his spine burned, but he accepted that ache,
that need, that Call of Magic and leaned into it. Accepting
everything being poured into him–body, mind, and soul–he
grew taller, wider, more than man, more than Dragon, he
was growing into the Winged Warrior he was meant to be.

In his mind's eyes, he saw the bones of his face twisting
and bending and morphing into a massive snout as the
plates of his skull expanded and separated. Sprouting on
either side of his head, enormous battle horns jutted toward
the sky and then curved backward with great, frightening
points. Joining in the Conversion from man to Dragon,
fighting spikes–smaller in the front and getting wider and
longer as they went–pushed through, forming at the center
of his head, flowing down his regal neck, and covering the
entire length of his spine and tail.

Before he could take stock of everything happening,
Cass was looking down from a twenty-foot height. Sensing
motion behind him, his huge head–led by his beautifully
audacious snout–turned to the side and watched the ten-
foot tail with a spaded end swish from side to side.

Suddenly, his body shook and the elongated muscles at
the center of what used to be his shoulders caught fire.
Instead of resisting, he again gave into the burn with the
knowledge that great things were to come.

And oh, they did...

Unfurling with grace and elegance far beyond anything he thought possible from a creature the size of his Dragon, wings with a span of sixty feet pushed forward and back. Flowing with and then against the gusty winds, the synchronicity of the moment was glorious.

Looking at Jed, Cass nodded his head and winked his mighty eye. The Black Stallion reared up on his hind legs, batted at the air with its front hooves and with a strong, loud neigh announced to all that he too had Shifted. He too had become what he was always meant to be.

Lifting off the ground, Cass snorted steam from King Blár's nostrils when Jed teased directly into his mind, *"Now that shit's just not fair."*

"Doesn't have to be fair."

"So says the guy with the wings."

"Just try to keep up, Lightning."

"I think I like that name. Although, I'd prefer you not call me Chief Crazy Horse," Jed laughed. Just then, the Black Stallion with whom he shared his soul voiced his definite disdain for the moniker in a thick Scottish Brogue. *"I am Vale, the Steed of the Isle, and I thank you to remember that."*

Laughing as he flew higher with every thrust of his wings, Cass lovingly taunted, *"Just try to keep up, Vale."*

And his Dragon King, just like Fate Herself, was not to be denied as he added, *"A race of the fittest in every way, Vale, Steed of the Isle."*

"I shall attempt to rise to the challenge, Blár, King of the Winter Dragons of Hope."

"Hey! Yo, Cass. You in there?"

The sharp rumble of Jed's voice, followed by a hand clamping onto his shoulder and shaking him with more than a little force, pulled Cass from his memories. Blinking his eyes, he stammered, "Wh-What happened? Did something...?"

"Yeah, something happened," his Aunt snapped. "You took a trip to La-La-Land and almost Shifted right here in my kitchen."

"Holy shit!" Eyes flying from Jed's to Barbara's, then back to Jed's, Cass ran his fingers through his hair and blew out a very long, very exasperated breath. "I don't... I mean, I shook your hand and... Well..." Fingers still tangled in the curls atop his head, he sighed. "I am so damned sorry, Aunt Barbara." Then, to Jed, he continued. "Honestly, I shook your hand, and it was like I went back in time."

"Back to when we first Shifted," Jed stated rather than asking.

Brows furrowing, Cass tried but failed not to growl, "Yeah, how did you know? Did you do that? Are you reading my mind? You know how I hate that shit."

Hands up in surrender, the Black Stallion Shifter vehemently shook his head and sternly attested, "Hell, no, I didn't read your mind, and I didn't cause you to take a trip down Memory Lane. Hell, I wouldn't fuck with somebody like that even if I didn't like them, I'd been interrogating them for seventy-two hours straight, and I hadn't slept in twice as long."

"Shit!" Hanging his hand, Cass went on, "I'm sorry." Meeting Jed's glare, he tried to lighten the mood. "Okay, there, Detective Chief Inspector of the Cherokee National Sheriff's Department, chill out. I'm not a perp. I didn't take the cookies from the cookie jar."

"Okay, you didn't have to..."

"Or should I have said, the newest Peace Chief of the Thorntree Wolf Tribe of the Cherokee Nation, and I didn't kiss your cousin behind the horse barn?"

"Aww, did ya' have to go and embarrass me?"

'You know I did," the Guardsman chuckled. "I had to spread it around. My face is gonna be red for a week. I need to share this shit, Especially since I tried to go all Dragon in the house."

"Yeah, that's right," Barbara scolded, trying to act tough even as the twinkle in her eye told another story. "You could've taken down the whole house. Then what would *y'all* have done if I hadn't been able to cook for the holidays? No ham, no mac-n-cheese, no little quiches... and not even a single cookie. What would you do?"

"Die!"

"Starve to death!"

Laughing when both men answered in unison with abject horror in their voices, she added, "That's right. So, be careful there, Kiddo." Patting Cass on the shoulder, she went on, "And just go find your Mate and get on with it. All the build-up is killin' me. Maybe you'll make me a Great Auntie. Now, that would be an awesome birthday present. You do remember that my birthday's in July, don'tcha?"

"Wait. Huh?" Feeling so confused, he thought he might have lost his hearing on his visit to the distant past, he sputtered, "Wh-What are *you* talking about?" Shrugging so vehemently that his shoulders almost met his earlobes, Cass looked at Jed, who was already doubled over in laughter, then back to his aunt, who was also chuckling. "No, seriously, what are y'all talkin' about?" When no answer came, he swatted the Stallion Shifter on the shoulder, then pushed even harder, "And how the hell did you know what was goin' on in my head?"

Pretty much falling into the chair behind him, Jed shoved back the long, dark hair that had fallen over his face, looked up, and nodded. "Well, since you seem to have forgotten, let me refresh your memory." Clapping his hands together, he rubbed them a couple of times, then said, "As Grandpa Cheveyo told us too long ago to think about, when we are close to meeting our Mate, to claiming her as our own and being claimed by her..." Stopping to clear his throat, when he began again, Jed sounded just like the Chief. "The time will come when you boys will remember the night in the Desert that the Great Celtic Dragon, King Alarick, and the Indigenous Deity, Begochiddy, spoke to each of you. It was under that Yuletide Full Moon that you, Jed, first heard the voice and felt the Magic of the Black Stallion with whom you share your soul, Vale."

Pausing, just as Cheveyo had so long ago, Jed slowly nodded before continuing. And you, Cass, well, you were very busy that night. Not only did you hear the voice of one of the Greatest Dragon Kings to ever fight alongside the Knights of Olde, the one who made it possible for the Guardsmen to exist by allowing the Great Mage to work his Magic, but you also heard the voice of your Dragon King, Blár and your Alpha Wolf, Faolan. As if that wasn't enough, you were given an honor that no other MacAllen Dragon, Thorntree Timber Wolf, or any other Shifter in our history has been given. Yes, dear boy, a grandson of my heart, you are the one and only among us who was ever given the choice between Dragon and Timber Wolf, but it doesn't end there. For you, Cass MacAllen, were also allowed to keep the soul of the Timber Wolf within you."

"I want you to very carefully remember everything that happened in the Desert that night, but only when the time is right. Years will pass when you will not even think of your first Shift or of that night when you first soared through the sky."

"However, when the day comes that your memories

demand your attention, when you recall these great events, you will know that you are on the cusp of finding your Mate. She will be nearer to you than she has ever been. Father Time will be counting the hours, the minutes until you will be with the one made for you by the Universe. The Bond you share with that special woman will grow strong. It will call to your mind. It will sing to your soul. It will prepare your heart for a love like no other. Know that when the vision of that blessed night returns, you will find the Light of your Soul, the Love of your life."

Getting closer, just as Cheveyo had, Jed nodded. "It will also be when you and the woman made for you by the Universe will be called upon to face your first and perhaps most monumental task as Mates. You will know the meaning of your Calling, of your Destiny as The Everlasting Hope."

"Well, shit," Cass breathed, following suit and falling into the nearest chair. "I had forgotten all about that. So, I'm...? I mean, she's...? No way. I would've...."

"Well, until this moment," his Aunt Barbara barked with laughter. "I would've said you could've finished a sentence hanging upside-down, underwater with a rag in your mouth, but apparently, finding out that what Bane told you is right, that you are about to meet your Mate, has shorted out your brain."

"Damn," the Dragon huffed. "I hate it when that happens."

5

With every step she took, the closer she got to the only home she'd ever known, and every single time the little butterflies in her tummy danced with excitement and joy. The Thorntree Reservation was special in so very many ways.

Sure, it was Magical. Everybody knew that. All a person had to do was get close to its borders, and they could feel how truly wonderful it was.

Yes, it was Sacred. It was the only indigenous land in the state of Texas that had always–*and would always*–belonged to the Cherokee people.

But what made it like no other place in the entire world, was all the people Abbie loved were there. The ones she held dear, the ones who she would do anything for, the people she would give her life to save, the Thorntree Res was where they lived.

It was home–and that word meant so much more than just a building. It truly was where her heart was, and for the first time, she could ever remember–something not quite right filled the air around the Res.

She couldn't put her finger on it, but with every step she took, the little voice in the back of her head screamed just a little bit louder. It refused to be ignored. Had it been corporeal, she had no doubt it would have also been jumping up and down, demanding her attention.

On one hand, she knew it wasn't the Timber She-Wolf with whom she shared her soul. It didn't matter that Abbie had never Shifted and probably never would. Faoiltiama–Faye, as she liked to be called, was always present and forever helping Abbie in any way she could. She was a gift from the Great Creator, the Universe, and most importantly, Abbie's dad.

On the other, she was starting to wonder if it might just be the Essence of the True Nûñně'hï Warrior she would someday become. She'd been told, and read many times that one day, one very specially ordained day, the true Spirit of the People Who Would Live Forever would be fully realized within her.

Abbie was also all too aware that if she hadn't found her Mate, their union hadn't been blessed by the Universe, and she didn't wear the Mating Mark of her Dragon by midnight on her birthday of her one hundred and twenty-fifth year she would become a Natural Nûñně'hï Warrior and therefore, she would be invisible. Sadly, Christmas Eve, that very special anniversary of the day Abigail Annabella Addams first saw the light of day, was just around the corner.

Shuffling through the many levels of her mind, all the hundreds of thousands of 'little boxes' she'd created over the years to keep things somewhat organized in her crazy brain, there was always the one she couldn't–or just didn't–open. It was the one that had been there from the very beginning. It was where the little voice–the loose interpretation of *Beannaichte Le Lomadh Spiorad* lived.

Explained by her dad's mom, Grandma Fione, *Bean-naichte Le Lomadh Spiorad* meant Blessed With Many Spirits, and only the most fortunate, most special, highly extraordinary people received those gifts from the Great Creator, the Universe, and all The Powers That Be. For the longest time, Abbie thought her Grandma, who was as Scottish as the day was long, was just biased because she was her Nana.

Then, the little box started to talk. Well, it didn't really talk. What it did was more like send out psychic vibrations that, for the first couple of months, had Abbie thinking she was losing her mind. After consulting with Grandma Mary and Momma Maybelle, the Tribal Medicine Woman and Elder of the Wisdom, she was happy to find out that she was not going crazy. She was a little less happy to learn that the 'little voice' was something she was going to have to learn to more than live with; she was going to have to coexist and sooner or later, talk back to.

So far, the conversing part hadn't happened. But what was occurring with more frequency were the times the box where the 'little voice' lived glowed, the times it shook, and the times–like the present–when that box vibrated like the washing machine during a spin cycle and little voice refused to be ignored.

Was it counting down to her birthday? Was it telling her she needed to have lunch? Was it..? Was it? Well, hell, was it telling her that her Dragon was nearby?

None of it made sense, especially the part about the man made for her by the Universe. And as of that very moment, she didn't know who or where her Mate was. That led her to wonder if she could live out eternity, not being seen by anyone or anything unless she chose to make herself known.

Some days, it sounded like a good thing. Most of the time, it scared the living shit right out of her. She figured with her luck, it would take her a millennium or two to figure out how to make herself seen, and by that time, well... She didn't want to think about it.

Snapping her out of her worries about the future, the little voice got so strong, so loud, so insistent that Abbie wondered if it might be time to take the lid off that specific box and see what all the hubbub was about. Would that speed up the deadline for her Mating? Would it change the way her Magic worked, who she was, or, most importantly, make her instantly invisible?

She just didn't know. But she was seriously thinking about throwing caution to the wind and going for it. Maybe meeting the little voice–or whatever was making all the noise–face to face would make things easier. It might even lead her to her Mate or, at the very least, call him to her.

But that felt all wrong. Somehow, and she didn't know how she just knew that it was not the right time to shake hands with the Essence of the Nûññë'hï. Her intuition was telling her that she had bigger fish to fry. That the little voice was so insistent because there was something much more pressing that needed her attention.

Then she remembered the weird feeling, the sense of something being not quite right, and she stopped mid-step. Laying her hand on Sydney's arm, she waited until her friend had also stopped, then asked, "Do you feel that? Can you...?"

"Oh, thank the Great Goddess," the blond blurted out, an expression of relief instantly falling over her face. "I thought it was just me–like maybe I was losing my mind or overre-acting to something nearby." Raising her eyebrows and bouncing her head, an action Abbie knew signaled that her friend was about to reveal something in confidence, some-thing she wouldn't tell almost anyone else, Sydney spilled, "I don't always have a good handle on what all the crazy Magic whipping around inside of me is trying to tell me. "Everyone keeps sayin' it's gonna take time to get used to, and they could *not* be more right. There were days that I thought something totally over the top, cuckoo-banana-pants-crazy, was about to happen. I was positive I needed to sound the alarm and make sure everyone took cover because the sky was falling. Cross my heart, you would've laughed your ass off as I ran around doing my best Chicken Little impression. I raced to Shavon, bolted through the huge Council doors without even knocking, and screamed, "All hell was about to break loose."

Huffing with such gusto that the blond curls framing her face flew up and then floated back into place, she continued. "Boy, did I feel foolish? First of all, every damn Oracle, Visionary, Prophesier, Other Elder, and all the rest were there. When it ended up being nothing more than some-body important–highly Magical or Mystical or something Otherworldly way over my pay grade–arriving at the Citadel–like the people in that very room, I was mortified."

"Oh, honey, I'm so sorry."

"Thanks, but that's not the worst. One time, I lost my ever–lovin' mind, and it was just the seasons being changed by the Enchantment of the Elemental Visionary on one of the other Realms." Shaking her head as a lovely pink blush colored her cheeks, she added, "Without Shavon or one of the other Oracles around to ask questions, I have pretty much learned to take a 'wait and see' approach. That way, I'm not embarrassed twenty-three-and-a-half hours out of twenty-four every day."

"Girl, I *so* hear ya'. I haven't run into a room with people like that, but I have yelled my fool head off more times than I like to admit. And I still have trouble sometimes, but it's *nothing* compared to what you got goin' on up in that cute curvy behind of yours." Pointing with both her index fingers, she wiggled them up and down, shimmied her shoulders, and winked. "I can't even imagine how all of your *Abracadabra-hoo-ha-woohoo* feels when something unfamiliar rubs up against it."

Twirling a stray red curl around the index finger of her right hand because it helped her think and gave her something to do with her hands, Abbie went on, "If I'm not puttin' my foot in my mouth, I'm missin' somethin' as obvious as the nose on my face, and I only have about point-zero-zero-zero-zero one percent of the Enchantment you have. So, the fact that you're still in one piece and so is the Refuge and the Citadel, says you are a freakin' rock star."

"Okay, yeah, whatever. You are one little powerhouse, Girlie. Don't you ever forget that. You are the first True and Natural Nûñnë'hï Warrior to walk the Earth in a *really, really* long time. Take some credit, my friend. Stop downplayin' your gifts."

"Well, I am not all the way a True and Natural Nûñnë'hï Warrior just yet and still don't completely comprehend all that that really means. Then there's the fact that there's still stuff that needs handlin'." Tilting her head to the side, she huffed a short breath. "Ya' know what I mean?"

"Oh, pfft, do not sweat the small stuff, and findin' your Dragon is small stuff. As a matter of fact, we'll start lookin' for your hunka-hunka-burnin' Winged Warrior right after we have coffee and sweets."

"Yeah, okay, if we get to it. Spendin' quality time with you is way more important than any man." Abbie tried to downplay the excitement she felt that Sydney was willing to help her find her Mate. She hadn't even thought about asking, but somehow, her friend always knew exactly what to say to make her feel better.

Then she remembered something Syd had just said, and she needed to add, "And I want you to know that I don't downplay my Gifts. I am *more* than thankful and grateful for each and every one of them. I just know what I've got goin' on, and I'm more than okay with that. I also know, 'cause I can feel it from a mile away, that you are wired for sound, and I am so damn proud to call you my friend."

"Right back atcha," Syd winked. "And for the record, I think we're both pretty damn awesome."

"You know it. We are all that and a big ass bag of chips. We even got the matching T-shirts." Snickering at her own joke and thinking about the ugly green and red Christmas shirts they'd gotten in place of ugly sweaters only last year, she added, "And while we're lookin' for my Dragon, we're gonna find yours too."

"Aww, thanks. I know Garrett's okay." She tapped her temple. "The Oracles keep tellin' me that I'll know when and if he needs me." Nodding, Syd's smile faltered as she got them back on track and asked, "So, what do you think this feeling is?" Holding up her arm, she pointed to the goosebumps. "These guys are dancing the Macarena, and the butterflies in my tummy are thinkin' about gettin' in on the act. It's close to the weirdest thing I've ever felt–and that's sayin' something, 'cause, in the last ten years, I have felt weirdness on a level I didn't know existed."

"Yeah, I know you have. And I feel the same heebie-jeebies you do," Abbie nodded. "I am so jumpy. It feels like I need to keep lookin' over my shoulder because something's comin' for me or someone close to me that should not be there. I absolutely hate this feeling, especially when I have no clue what it is or where it's coming from."

"Ditto."

"All I can be sure of is that something is way over-the-top cattywampus, and it's not gonna get fixed all by itself." Stopping to think for a second, she snapped her fingers when an idea hit her. "Let me holler at Auggie. She is pretty much *always* at the Res, and the eeriness seems to be floating from that direction." She pointed to the west.

"Yep, sure does."

Nodding in agreement, Abbie continued, "You know as well as I do that Auggie only leaves home if she's forced. Even then, she makes a big fuss and threatens to curse anyone in her path even though I'm pretty sure the worst she could do is Shift into her Timber Wolf and bite 'em in the butt." Shrugging, she winked. "She says everything she needs is right there, and home is where she wants to be. So, it only stands to reason that if anything is goin' on, Cuz will for sure have a handle on it. I'll find out what she knows. That way, if everything's good and we've just gotten our wires crossed, we won't have alerted anyone else, and I won't get accused of havin' a crazy imagination *again*."

"If your imagination is crazy, then mine is nuckin' futs. So, go on ahead and holler for Miss Augustine. She's always had the answers before."

Without further comment, Abbie opened the unique mental connection she shared with her cousin, and as cheerfully as she could so as not to alert Auggie to anything nefarious, she sing-songed and called her cousin the one name she truly hated. *"Hey, Miss Thang, whatcha doin?"*

Waiting for an answer, an exasperated sigh, or anything that said Auggie had heard her was like the anxiety she experienced while sitting in the dentist's chair anticipating having a tooth pulled. It was almost as painful as the act itself–and it required a patience she did not have.

When no response came, she tried again, *"Hey, Auggie, guess who's here? Sydney! We're headed to my house for leftover chicken and dumplings, followed by coffee, cookies, and silly holiday rom coms. I even paid for the Hallmark Channel after you got mad about me using yours. Can you believe it? I actually have a subscription in my own name. You wanna join the party? Aww, come on, you just gotta. You'll finally get to watch something I paid for."*

Again, she waited. Again, there was no answer, but this time, Abbie was quickly running out of what little patience she had–which wasn't much. It was so bad, and the little voice in the back of her mind was pushing so hard that her feet had already started creeping toward the Res.

Ready to add some oomph to her voice and try not to yell even though it was all she could think about doing, she got as far as, *"Okay, Aug, what's...?"*

"D-don't don't c-come home. N-not not s-safe." Auggie's voice was barely a whisper–actually a breathy wheeze–that had every protective instinct and need to help and heal Abbie possessed jumping to the forefront of her psyche. Then her cousin added, *"C-can-can't co-come h-here. B-be s-s-safe,"* and her feet went from barely shuffling to beatin' a trail to the Res before her brain caught up.

"Come on, Syd. The shit's hittin' the fan!" She hollered into the wind without so much as a backward glance, trusting her friend to follow along.

"I'm right behind you!"

With her bestie hot on her trail, their footfalls pounding the ground like a herd of raging heifers, Abbie shoved her hands out in front of her chest. Hitting the gate at the back of her garden with a blast of Magic that almost knocked it off its hinges, she raced under the white, wrought iron arch covered with flowering white ivy and yellow Carolina jessamine in full bloom. No sooner was she through than she really poured on the speed.

Around the side of her house, just barely missing the purple Texas sage and yellow and red hibiscus bushes trying to take over her yard, she took a sharp right then jumped over the rocks from the creek she used as stepping stones like she was playing hopscotch. Through her Auntie's backyard, she kicked open the wooden gate to Auggie's yard and ran full speed for the sliding glass door.

Ready to push it open with her Magic, the glass was already moving, and Syd was calling out, "I got this one. Don't want you shattering glass like you tore up that hinge, Wreckin' Ralph," before she hopped up on the redwood deck.

"Ha," was all Abbie could force through her gritted teeth as the bittersweet sour scent of sickness and the cloyingly overpowering stench of pain invaded her senses and then shot through her system so quickly there was no time for her to do anything but brace for what was to come.

Coughing with such force that her eyes watered and she couldn't catch her breath, she stopped just inside the kitchen. Forced to hold onto the dark, Mahogony crown molding around the threshold to stay upright, she panted as if she'd just run a marathon—something that would never happen.

The Magic of the Nûñnë'hï combined with that of her Timber She-Wolf and instantly went to work. Sweeping through her system, it wiped away almost all of the offensive odor and allowed her to take one quick, cleansing breath. Finally, and way quicker than she'd ever imagined, she was able to block out what little of the offensive stench remained and take a second, deeper inhale. Wiping away the tears wetting her cheeks, she stood up to her full height just as Sydney rushed past.

Running when her friend gasped, "Holy Goddess," Abbie dashed into Auggie's room, stopping so quickly that her body swayed forward and then back. She simply couldn't believe what she saw. It made no sense. It was like something out of a horror movie.

The tall, brunette Augustine Addams, usually so full of life, always sassy, and absolutely drop-dead gorgeous, was laid out flat, tangled in a mess of sheets wet with sweat and stained with throw-up, looking worse than death warmed over. Her eyes were rolled so far back in her head that only the tiniest speck of her dark brown eyes was visible, and her long, beautiful brunette tresses were drenched with perspiration, stringy and matted on her pillow that was also sopping.

Abbie tried not to gasp as she took in Auggie's usually soft, flawless, olive complexion that was at that moment horribly mottled and washed out to a dreary gray pallor, but she failed. Then, the worst happened. The moment she watched the way her cousin's chest barely rose and fell as she struggled to breathe, the life was sacred out of Abbie, and her heart ached as if it had been stabbed.

The closer she got, the more glaringly obvious it became that whatever was attacking her cousin most definitely defied all the Laws of Nature. It had happened too fast. Nothing, no matter how infectious or life-threatening–worked that quickly. She had just seen Auggie that morning, and the older-by-three-years-old woman was fine, happy, healthy, and giving her hell for something she'd forgotten to do.

Not to mention, Auggie was a Timber She-Wolf–one

who had already accepted her Magic from the Universe and Shifted under the cool Yuletide Full Moon the day she turned sixteen. There was no way anything of the Earth could have caused the sudden downturn Abbie witnessed. Nothing could've gotten past the Timber Wolf Enchantment or the Indigenous Magic of the Cherokee. Auggie was to be a Luna when she found her Mate. She would have her own Pack, maybe her own Tribe someday.

What Abbie witnessed was impossible. She wouldn't have believed it if she wasn't seeing with her own eyes, and still, it just didn't make any sense.

The disease, the sickness, the attack had to be wicked or malevolent or both. That was the only explanation for the lack of healing taking place within her cousin's body. The Timber She-Wolf with whom she shared her soul would've taken over and done her damnedest to rush Auggie to her glowing health immediately.

Trying to reach out to the Timber She-Wolf, Fatima, who shared her very essence with Auggie, Abbie found all mental pathways blocked. She went one way and then another, trying to get in there to see what had happened, but it was no use. Fati had been silenced. She was under house arrest, and not even the Magic of the Nûññë'hï could break the lock.

Taking in the icky green pustules on Auggie's eyelids, lips, and the inside of her nose, Abbie's stomach rolled. Then she saw the red, fiery tendrils snaking their way up and down her body and knew her cousin's symptoms were unlike anything she'd ever studied in college.

Sure, she'd gotten her degree in photography, but that didn't mean she hadn't taken a ton of biology, physiology, anatomy, and other sciences. After all, she was about to be one-hundred-and-twenty-five, and that meant she'd had a lot of time on her hands. It also helped her understand bodies, how they moved, and the best way to get the right pictures when working with humans–which wasn't often but did sometimes happen.

Looking around, trying to find any physical evidence of what was happening to her cousin, she was just about to give up when the feeling of pure evil damn near smacked her in the face. There was no denying it. Someone, no, *something* had infected Auggie with the nastiest, blackest Magic she'd ever felt. The sheer magnitude of the warped alchemy permeating the airwaves was staggering. So, why hadn't she...?

"You did not feel it when we first entered the house because it was being hidden," Faye answered. *"Not even I can get through all the blockages and blind alleys this Maliciousness is causing. It is absolutely infuriating, unbelievably strong, and Ancient. There is no doubt that it's Otherworldly, but I can't tell from where."*

"Wow, did you just wake up?"

"No need to be snippy, Isi. I have been in meditation, seeking answers for what is to come. I thought we should be prepared to meet your Mate as the time is drawing near."

"Okay, I'm sure that's important, but do you have to call me Little One every time I say something you don't particularly like?"

"I do, and sometimes I do it just because I can."

"Well, what can we...?"

Not waiting for Abbie to finish her question or even so much as give her consent, Faye opened their minds to everyone in the Tribe. Pushing through the wall, the one wielding the Black Magic had haphazardly built around Auggie's house, her innate Nûññë'hï Magic lent its Second Sight, and as one, they all checked on Abbie's Family, her Tribe.

Slapping her in the face, what she found was even worse than she'd imagined. It was more of the same and, in some cases, much worse. Everyone, the old, the young, the strong, and those who needed a helping hand, were being attacked by the horrific, malevolent sickness. Whether they had just started to feel poorly or if they were as bad off as Auggie, every single person on the Thorntree Res was under siege from the gruesome, wicked illness.

Turning, she asked, "Syd, do you mind stayin' with Auggie?"

"Not at all. I caught most of what y'all said and what you saw. I wasn't eavesdropping. Y'all just weren't shielding."

"No worries," Abbie nodded. "You know you are always free to eavesdrop in my crazy brain. Just enter at your own risk."

"Cool, I just gotta ask, are you goin' where I think you're goin'?"

"Probably," Abbie confirmed. "I'm going out to Sequoyah Hill."

"Yep, I got it in one."

"'Cause you know me so well." Abbie forced half a smile. "I was able to see everyone in the Tribe who should be on the Res, but Cheveyo and Momma Maybelle. For some reason, I couldn't even sense them. There was a hole where they should've been—their places in my Mind's Eye, in my heart, and in my soul. It's just empty. Then, when I used the bond I shared with only them, it was dark and solitary, just not... Well, it just wasn't there. It's like we somehow got unplugged from one another, and I couldn't find the outlet or the cord."

"Go," the blond insisted. "You gotta find them if we're gonna get to the bottom of all of this and help everyone. I'll see what I can do to ease Auggie's pain. I've done quite a bit of training with the Elemental Healers at the Citadel. I might not be able to completely rid her of this infection because it's rotten to the core, but I'm pretty sure I can help."

"Go for it! I appreciate anything you can do."

With no time to spare and not wanting to run because it was her least favorite activity in the whole wide world any longer, Abbie flashed to the two-story red brick house with a wraparound porch, white sills, and black shutters sitting atop Sequoyah Hill. It was and always had been Cheveyo's home. Appearing out of the Ether with her feet on the steps to the entrance of the house, she stood perfectly still.

Something was really, really wrong. The front door was standing wide open. Sure, it was common knowledge that the Chief never locked his door, but he never left it open either. If there was one thing a person could count on in Texas, especially the Chihuahuan Desert, it was critters of the buggy, pinchy, and basically yucky variety outnumbering everything else a hundred to one. That was why pretty much every house had screens, and no one left doors or windows open if they could help it.

With one foot over the threshold, she yelled, even though she was certain there was no one there. "Hey, Cheveyo! It's Abigail. You here?"

Waiting for precisely one heartbeat, she pushed her Enchantment in every direction within the walls of the home just to double-check that it was indeed empty. When she was sure she was alone, Abbie went through the dining room and kitchen and then out the backdoor. The minute the warm, dry breeze hit her cheeks she flashed to Momma Maybelle's cottage on the opposite side of the Res.

Atop Raintree Hill sat the one-story ranch-style cottage. Bright white with red shutters and a white picket fence, there was every flower, herb, and medicinal plane ever known to man and a few no one had ever heard of and never would. A familiar and welcoming creak filled the air as the wind blew the antique rocking chairs back and forth on the perfectly appointed porch. Momma Maybelle called it her little slice of Heaven, and Abbie agreed.

But on this occasion, things were very different. Something had soiled the safest place on the Res and pissed Abbie off as nothing ever had.

Once again, no one was home. Once again, she Magically checked every nook and cranny. Then, when she was about to leave through the side door, her gaze lit upon three tiny words scratched in the white baseboard behind the kitchen door: *Find your Uktena.*

"How did she...?" Shaking her head as she turned to leave, Abbie answered with a forced snicker, "Because she's Momma Maybelle."

"And because she is the oldest and wisest Medicine Woman to ever live. That's why she is the one and only Elder of the Wisdom as appointed by the Great Creator," Faye added. *"That's how she knew you would be the one coming to find her, and you would know to look for any clues she might have left behind. After all, she is also the Keeper of the Eternal Lunar Light and the great-grandmother to the renowned Cherokee Chief John Ross. She can damn near do anything."*

"Still freaks me out sometimes."

Flashing back to Auggie's house, she was glad to see a tiny bit of color returning to her cousin's face. Whatever Sydney was doing was working, and that was the best news she could have gotten.

Sitting in the chair next to the bed, Abbie held her cousin's hand and mentally asked Sydney, *"Has her temperature come down at all? It still feels like she's on fire."*

Before the blond could answer, Auggie groaned through

gritted teeth, "Don't talk about me like I'm not here. I can still whoop your butt if I need to."

"Okay, Tiger, I know you're tough."

"Damn straight." Wheezing then gasping, Auggie coughed and hacked, the sound gut-wrenching and heart-breaking.

Grabbing a cool, wet cloth to wipe her cousin's forehead, Abbie hoped it would lower her temperature even a degree. Just barely opening her eyes, Auggie whispered, "No, my fever has not come down, and if you think I feel hot to the touch, you oughta be in here."

Snorting a chuckle despite the worry beating at her soul, Abbie joked, "You always were the hot one."

"Says the girl with flaming red c-c-." But that was as far as Auggie got before she again coughed and hacked, then gagged. Convulsing every time her lungs forcefully expelled air, Abbie just barely kept her cousin from rolling off the bed. Harder and harder, she coughed until bloody phlegm flew from her lips, decorating everything in its path in bright red and green splatters.

With her lips turning blue and only the whites of her eyes showing, Auggie coughed and barked until there was nothing left. Collapsing onto the bed, unconscious and once again struggling to breathe, she was so frail, so incredibly pale, that Abbie feared the worst.

"Dammit!" Syd spat, jumping to her feet and pacing the floor. "I thought it was working. I did everything I could. I spoke to Bane, and he told me what he knew, promising he'd get here as soon as he could."

Wringing her hands and pacing from one end of the room to the other, she continued, "Then I called Dian, the Oracle Physician, the one with the ability to tap into the Primordial

Healing Magic of the Earthly Realm to help Earthly bound Healers restore others." Waving at the air as if she were erasing a chalkboard, she hurried on, "Sorry. What she is and what she does is of no consequence. What is important is that I did exactly what she told me to do. I followed all the steps, said all the right words, and pulled from the Magic of the Earth." Stopping midstride, she turned, motioned with both hands toward the woman in bed, and kept right on going, "And Auggie was getting better. You saw it. She was really gettin' better. So, what happened? Why is she...?"

The pounding of thundering hooves filled Abbie's consciousness. It was all she could hear. It demanded her attention. It refused to be ignored. It was even louder than the 'little voice.' Her heart even beat in the same rhythm. Vision blurring and ears ringing, sounds of something large and vindictive coming straight for her grew louder with every passing second.

Trying to focus on Sydney, to hear what she was saying, to see more than a billowy shadow through the thick, black fog filtering in from every direction, Abbie opened her mouth to speak only to have the words blown back in her face. She tried to step in front of the blond, but her feet wouldn't move. Finally, she did the only thing she could think of—she raised her hands over her head, waved them all around, and jumped up and down.

Still nothing.

The conclusion she reached, the solitary thing that made any sense at all, was that she was the only one who could see and hear the signs of impending doom, and she was getting her first glimpse at what it would be like to be invisible—and that shit would not stand. She had to try to make Sydney see what was happening. There had to be a way. She couldn't stand idly by and let her friend, her cousin, or anyone else get hurt.

Trying a move that had won the Girls' Basketball Finals in her senior year in high school, Abbie leaned one way, then stepped the other, then tried with all her might to zig-zag through the intertwining, hazy plumes. As soon as she'd made the littlest bit of headway, she shoved her arms through the wall of fog and reached for Sydney. Sadly, she pulled back a handful of rotten flesh and dead vines from the grape arbors around the Res.

Again and again, she tried, and every time the same thing happened. Sydney continued to pace and explain how she was trying to help Auggie, and Auggie lay there struggling to breathe. It was time to call out the big guns.

Turning her Second Sight inward, she fought through the haze with a single-minded determination, refusing to be thwarted. Pouring all the Magic, Nûññë'hï, Timber She-Wolf, and Healing Enchantment she'd inherited from her dad's dad, Papa Dayfedd, a Celtic Shaman she could summon, Abbie pulled an ancient Cherokee War Club from the Ether and started beating away at the wall of mist and muck before her.

Her muscles were on fire. She thought her arms might actually fall off, but she refused to give up. Punching through the pea soup hanging in the air all around her, she shouted with all her might for Sydney to pay attention and realize what was happening.

Nothing worked. Still, the thundering hooves grew closer and closer. Still, every sense she possessed was screaming for her to fight. Still, the 'little voice' demanded she pay attention to what it was trying to say.

Faye growled, *"Never give up, Isi. Fight! Fight hard! You*

must get to the other side. You must destroy whoever or whatever is causing this disruption to the fabric of the Earth."

"*You can do this,*" the voice of the Ditlihi commanded. "*As you are Abigail Addams, you are more than the Great Creator's Chosen Warrior. You are a Warrior of Light. You are Beloved. You are the Hope. Do what you were meant to do.*"

Tucking the shaft of the elaborately hand-carved War Club under her arm, she choked up on the shank with her right hand. Reaching across her body with her left, she hooked her pinky finger on the edge of the socket, pointing the heavy ball-shaped head with spikes made of bone, stone, and metal at the threat barreling toward her, and spread her feet shoulder-width apart.

With a slight bend of her knees, she pulled every ounce of power and strength she had into her core and inhaled deeply. Holding her breath, counting every strike of hooves against the ground, she exhaled slowly.

Shadows, long and dark, shimmered through the thick, dense fog. At first, they looked like long, gnarled fingers reaching out for her, beckoning her to trust when her every instinct told her to do the exact opposite.

Floating in the mist, they twisted and turned, bending and buckling into a broken outline, a dotted line that made no sense at all. It was no form she recognized. It was disjointed and malformed, appearing as random pieces of a jigsaw with no end, no beginning, no middle, and absolutely no hope of ever fitting together.

The longer she stood at the ready, the darker the scattered bits grew. They gained substance. They took the shape of something far scarier than anything she could have dreamed of in any nightmare.

The shadowy figure appeared to be upwards of thirteen feet tall. She only knew that because she'd helped Auggie remodel her house, and those ceilings had been a bitch to paint. Coming in at fourteen feet, they were some of the tallest in the Res, and Abbie, one the shortest, had been nominated to stand on the ladder and man the roller. It was something she wouldn't soon forget.

Watching as the sharp, pointed tip of the triangular blade of an incredibly ornate Ceremonial Tomahawk raised high left a glaring crevice where it scraped the ceiling, she thought about yelling, "Hey, Asshole! You gonna repaint that?"

But then her eyes followed the straight wooden handle that led to the rider's left hand and couldn't stop as she took in the twisted and curvy line of the blood-stained, skeletal arm disappearing into the thick black cloak of the creature riding the most grotesque horse she'd ever seen, and words failed her. Unable to stop her gaze from wandering, no matter how hard she tried and how much she didn't want to see anymore, she locked eyes with what had to have been a horse at one point in time, and her stomach turned.

Crimson eyes, the color of fresh-spilled blood with the Fires of Hell burning in their soulless depths, told the story of an unending torment that was far worse than any of the stories she'd been told. Bits of putrid flesh and foul gore hung from the tips of the huge, uneven fangs left bare by the lack of flesh and fur.

Legends of the Skeletal Horse were told by harsh parents to warn naughty children to mind their Elders and eat their vegetables. For the adults, *Deid Cuddie*–the Dead Horse–was more than a myth. It was the foretelling of the coming of the End of Days. It was the creature they'd been taught about from the Celtic Dragons, who they'd welcomed onto their land and into their Reservation. It was the Beast of Burden she'd heard about all of her life...

But what galloped toward her was far worse than anything her grannies, Auntie, uncles, grandpas, and even the Chiefs and Elders of her Tribe had described. What was barreling at an unnatural speed in her direction could only be powered by Black Magic at the hands of an Incredible Evil, and it scared the crap out of her.

Nineteen hands high at the tip of its withers, for the most part, the *Deid Cuddie* was nothing but bones. It pretty much looked like the creature from her imagination, but that's where the similarity ended. Everything was made so much worse by the ragged pieces of fetid flesh, moldy strings of what had to have been muscles and connective tissue and globules of rancid blood hanging from every crack, notch, and rounded growth–especially each and every joint that it had.

"That horse is fuckin'... fuckin'.... It has fuckin' fangs. Nobody ever said the horse had fangs. Why didn't they tell me?" The words, her words, floated through her mind to Faye's and the Ditlihi's just as her eyes met the rider's, and her blood ran cold.

Black as night, they were so dark they were the epitome of nothingness. More than soulless, they were vacuous with a pull that reached into the depths of Abbie's very essence, latched their vicious claws into the pulp of her existence, and tried with aberrant strength to absorb her very life.

Gaunt, almost skeletal, the rider's face had more form than *Deid Cuddie* with transparent, wafer-thin skin showcasing the black and purple veins slithering and writing as they pumped the viscous fluid that kept the rider upright. There was no nose, or it was hidden in the shadows cast by the hood. Abbie couldn't tell. And honestly, didn't want to know. All she knew for sure was that whatever was sitting atop the Dead Horse made her skin crawl.

Then it happened. The rider realized she was there. Their eyes locked. The rider's head snapped to the left and then whipped back to the right.

What was it looking for? Was it getting the lay of the land? Was it surveying the torment it was inflicting upon the Tribe? And who the hell was the rider? She'd never heard a story in which *Deid Cuddie* had a rider.

Tired of waiting, sick of the anticipation, needing to do something–anything–she yelled, "Who the fuck are...?"

Swinging back to the front, the rider's jaw dropped to its chest, its head fell backward, and the air filled with an unearthly shriek that made the hair all over Abbie's body stand on end. As quickly as it started, the sound stopped, but the echo continued.

Head popping back up, the sound of cracking bones replaced the screech as the rider's hood slid backward. Abject horror and total disbelief had Abbie's hands tightening around the handle of the War Club as she gasped, *"No fuckin' way!"*

"Your eyes do not deceive you, Isi," Faye confirmed. *"The rider is female. She is..."*

"Uya," Abbie, the Timber She-Wolf, and the Ditlihi snarled.

A plethora of emotions, too many to count or identify, washed over, around, and through her. Callous, cold, and cruel, the rider was indeed the Uya–the evil Earth Spirit who opposed everything good and right in the world. If the *Deid Cuddie* was the stuff of childhood nightmares, then the Uya was every person's worst fear, deepest dread, and what could literally keep them up at night, all rolled into one.

Within the Uya, there was no spark of Life or Light. There wasn't even Darkness. There was quite literally nothing.

She did not feel. She did not want to. She did not think, at least not as any living being would understand those things. The Uya only acted on the instinct given to her at the time of her inception–which was always by a twist of Black Magic and a demented Practitioner of the Dark Arts.

No one knew who created the Uya, only that she existed to rob the world of Light in all its many forms. She was a Destroyer who did her job with extreme prejudice, accepting nothing but the complete annihilation of anything just, right, or good that stood in her way.

She acted upon a person's worst fears. She projected what she wanted her victims to feel to make them weak, to control them, and then she took them to the brink of madness. Once there, she feasted on the delusion, the delirium, and the hysteria until there was nothing left but an empty husk.

Everything within the Uya was feral, insensitive, and subhuman. Her unquenchable desire to consume, warp, and defile everything in her path was incomprehensible for any living being to understand. Or so Abbie thought until that very moment. In a split second, she'd looked into the Uya's soulless eyes. She knew everything she needed to know–the Uya had to go, and she had to be the one to do it.

"It's why I am here." The words floated from her mind to Faye and the Ditlihi.

With every shield, mental block, and shred of protection she had, Abbie refused to back down. There could be no weakness. That was what the Uya wanted. She needed a place to plant the seed of her malice, cruelty, and spite into Abbie. She wanted to fill her up with anything and everything that would erase even the smallest shred of decency and goodness she possessed. She wanted the Spirit of the Nûñnë'hi and everything it represented. She wanted to warp the beautifully perfect loving and healing Nature of the People Who Would Live Forever and kill it. She wanted to turn Abbie into a tool, a weapon that could be turned on the world.

Quite simply, the Uya wanted to kill Hope.

"Focus, Abigail," the voice of the Ditlihi commanded, *"Concentrate on the Light. Find your center. Hold your ground. Then, when you are ready, take in the rest of the Uya."*

"But I..."

"I know you don't want to see it–to see her–but you must. For to defeat your enemy, you must know your enemy. To destroy the Darkness, you must know where to shine the Light."

Feeling the infusion of Ancient Indigenous Magic and the Love and Kinship of the Ancient Cherokee, Abbie pictured her mom and dad. She thought about the stories she'd heard. She remembered what the Ditlihi had told her about the night of the Clash at Guadalupe Peak and how bravely they'd given all they had–even their very lives–to do the right thing, to save the people they loved and, most of all, to give their only daughter the best chance at life.

"This one's for you, Agitsi and Agidoda," she whispered, speaking mother and father in the Cherokee language. *"I just hope I can be as brave as you were."*

Forcing her eyes upward, she refused to gasp. She would not give the Uya the satisfaction of knowing how scared she truly was. Her parents had been strong. Her grandparents before them had been Warriors. Abbie's entire lineage was filled with those who had defied the odds, had reached deep inside themselves, and found the will to stand up against a force that seemed far more powerful than they themselves were.

Once again, she met the Uya's gaze, but she looked up and instantly wished she hadn't. The Evil Earth Spirt had no hair; instead, her skull was covered with a writhing mass of inky black and oily green tentacles with gaping maws, thin and gray bifurcated tongues, and ragged incisors dripping with a venom that popped and sizzled when it hit the floor.

"Holy crap! Is she Medusa's sister? Please tell me she's not Medusa's sister. I won't look good turned to stone. I think I'd rather be invisible."

"No, Isi," Faye reassured. *"The Uya is not kin to the Gorgon Queen."*

As she first imagined, the Uya had no nose, nor did she have lips, just a mouth full of sharp, jagged canines that were brownish-yellow and filled with gore and carnage. Her chin was elongated and pointed and reminded Abbie of the blade of the ceremonial dagger that hung over the fireplace in Cheveyo's office.

Committing every detail of her enemy to memory, the stories, the legends, and the information her Elders had shared with her over the years returned. She heard her mom's mom–Grandma Cassie's voice loud and clear, "The Uya resulted from the Hatred, the Darkness, the Despair created when the chaos of war and famine were allowed to run wild. She sprung from the wasteland left behind when pure Evil was allowed to run amuck–even for a short period of time. She is ancient, almost as old as the Earth, and she wants it all to die."

Then her Grandpa Johnny spoke, picking up where her grandma had stopped. "At first, the Great Creator and the Powers That Be believed the Uya was necessary. They saw her as a way to help people. They wanted people to understand the duality and potential danger of negative forces in the world. You see, Isi, without Darkness, there can be no Light. Without Evil, there can be no Good. We–the normal folk–have to have both. We have to know both to recognize the difference."

"The trick is the balance," Momma Maybelle began. "Even you, a child born of the Light, must know Darkness. You must see the Evil but not be a part of it because you, Abigail Annabella Addams, like all of your Family, are Good. There are few better. You, Isi, are the Hope."

Letting out the breath she hadn't realized she was holding, Abbie fanned her fingers as they held onto the handle of the War Club to get the blood flowing and stood her ground. In the cavernous nothingness of the Uya's eyes, she recognized the machinations of true Malice. The Evil Earth Spirit was formulating her plan of attack. There it was, plain as day, as her eyes shifted from Abbie to the right.

The Uya knew Sydney was there and recognized the prize both women were.

Without another thought, Abbie slid in front of her friend and her cousin, yelling, "You came here for me, Bitch. So, let's do this!"

Roaring, the sound so piercing and unearthly that Abbie could literally feel her eardrums vibrating, the Uya spoke its first words, "I will have you, Abigail Annabella Addams."

Tuning out as she continued to pull fortitude from the center of the Earth, from Mother Nature Herself, Abbie tuned back in just as the Uya boasted, "But first, I will have all you hold dear–your friend, your family, and your Uktena. Today is the day of your death. Today is the death of the Everlasting Hope!"

Opening her mouth to once again challenge the Evil Earth Spirt, a deep, rumbling voice burst into her mind, "*Hold on, Mo stór! From this day forward, we fight side by side!*"

6

Slowly taking a bite out of the third, or maybe it was the fourth cookie since his cousin's shocking revelation, Cass had just wrapped his fingers around the handle of his mug when Barbara speared him with a look and started poking and prodding. "You know I don't care how many cookies you eat. Hell, I'll start bakin' more right this very minute if you were eatin' them to enjoy 'em and not just because you're stallin'. Leaning her hip against the counter, she continued, gaining conviction with every word. "You know it. I know it. Jed knows it. Everybody knows it. It's been your go-to play since you were a little boy."

"Yep," his cousin chimed in with a smirk on his face, a twinkle in his eye, and a cookie in his hand. "Sure has."

"Traitor."

"Dude, the most amazin' auntie in all the world speaks the truth. Just because I agree does not make me a traitor."

"And this boy right here..." Pushing off the counter, Barbara took the three steps to get to Jed's side and patted him on the shoulder with the biggest smile on her face. "...is not a traitor. He just knows what I'm sayin' is right, as usual."

"Absolutely," his cousin nodded emphatically. "The woman speaks the truth."

"Argh," Cass growled, setting his mug back on the table before getting any coffee. He shoved his fingers through his hair. He could feel every curl standing at attention atop his head but just couldn't care. His aunt and cousin were right, and he hated that they were right, but not even his disgust at the situation changed the fact that... They. Were. Right.

With a single sharp shake of his head, he growled under his breath one more time about know-it-all relatives and other such things, smacked his knee with the palm of his hand, and got to his feet. Reaching over, he grabbed his hat off the far end of the table, slammed it on his head, and glared first at his cousin, then, after softening his gaze to a light glower, looked at his aunt. Huffing out a sharp breath, he closed his eyes and centered himself so he wouldn't snarl at one of his favorite people in the whole world.

Opening his eyes, he watched Barbara's smile brighten, and the love in her eyes multiply by leaps and bounds. Across the kitchen in the blink of an eye. She pushed up on her toes, wrapped her arms around his neck, and pulled him down into a hug. "You're gonna be just fine, Son."

Patting him, she moved backward, kissing him on the cheek as she went. The second he was looking into her twinkling eyes, she reassured, "You got this, Cass, my boy. You were made for this, and so was she. She is your Mate. The woman the Universe made for you. She is the other half of your soul and the Light to your Darkness. You know what you gotta do. Go see Grandad Cheveyo. You know he's got all the answers you need."

"And if he doesn't," Jed added. "Momma Maybelle is there, too." Popping half a cookie that used to be the shape of a snowman decorated with icing and sprinkles into his mouth, he continued as he chewed. "You know they've got all the answers you could ever want and then some."

"And you know that you're not supposed to talk with a mouth full," Barbara grumped, having turned so she could look at both men. Shoulders bouncing as she tried to hold back her chuckles, she added, "And don't you think you should be goin' with your cousin?"

Swallowing as quickly as possible, then downing an entire glass of milk, the Stallion Shifter shook his head so vigorously that his long, dark hair swept around hm like a cape. "No, ma'am. I came here to talk to you then got..."

"You got distracted by food," Cass deadpanned, knowing he had a look of disgust on his face. "Don't you even try to convince me that you got distracted because I was here. We all know how you love sweets. The whole of the great state of Texas knows how you love baked goodies. Wouldn't ya' just know it? I get sold out for cookies, milk, and Aunt Barb's conversation."

"Damn straight!" Jed cheered, then popped yet another cookie in his mouth. Making a show of chewing with his mouth shut, he teased telepathically, *"Go on now, Son. Time to get a move on. You need to go see a Chief about a Mate."*

"And you need to shut up."

"I swear to the Heavens," Barbara chuckled. "It's just like old times when you two get together–bicker, makeup, bicker, makeup, bicker, makeup. How old are y'all again?"

"Old enough to know better," they answered in unison before bursting out with laughter that filled the entire house. Then Jed added, "And just think, pretty soon, everybody will be here. Talk about lettin' the good times roll."

The laughter was boisterous and so wonderful that Cass almost forgot what he was about to do.

Just almost...

No sooner had the hilarity calmed than he leaned down, kissed his auntie on the cheek, and then nodded to his cousin. "Alright," he sighed. "I'm gonna head out." Raising his eyebrows, he attempted to coax, "You sure you don't want to come along, Jed. I sure could use a Wingman."

"Nope, Dude. This is all you," the Stallion Shifter winked. "Besides, I really need to...."

"Talk to Aunt Barb, yeah, yeah, yeah..." Cass pretended to be irritated. "Just know that I'm not buyin' a word of it, and paybacks are a bitch."

"Duly noted, Cuz. Duly noted," Jed snickered.

Heading for the backdoor, Cass hollered over his shoulder with a snicker, "Oh yeah, love you both."

"And we love you," Aunt Barbara sing-songed. "Now, hurry up and bring your Mate back. I think a Mating Ceremony is the perfect way to celebrate the Holidays!"

"I'll do my best."

Out the door, down the steps, and through his favorite aunt's flower garden, he was across the edge of the Chihuahuan Desert closest to the MacAllen Ranch and into McKittrick Canyon in the blink of an eye. Inhaling all the scents and sounds that were uniquely home, he stopped to pick up a few flat rocks and skip them across the babbling waters of the creek while trying to get his thoughts in order.

"It won't do for us to show up over there and not have all our ducks in a row," he explained to Blár.

"No, it will not," the Dragon King with whom he shared his soul agreed. *"Cheveyo does not suffer fools. Then again, there isn't much to get ready. You know what you must do."* Blár paused, and Cass could feel him thinking. Finally, he continued, *"Tell him that you remembered what he'd told you the night of our first Shift, and you need his help finding the signs that will lead to your Mate."*

"*You know, none of my cousins had to go to Cheveyo to find their Mate. Do you really think...?*"

"*Yes, I really think that every prophecy, prediction, and conversation you have had since that first Shift has led us to this place, at this time, to the Great Chief of the Thorntree Tribe to not only receive your blessing but to allow him to point you in the right direction.*"

"*But...*"

"*But nothing, Lad. Bane told you, and now Jed has confirmed that time is short. The clock is ticking. For some reason, there is an expiration date stamped on your arse, and you need to find your Mate sooner rather than later. So, in the words of your very wise Aunt Barbara, it's time to get a move on.*"

"*Yeah, well...*"

Letting his words wander as he watched a Mule Deer Doe coax her twin Fawns across the meadow on the opposite side of the stream, Cass thought about what it would be like to have a family–a Mate and children of his own. As soon as the thought popped into existence, Blár, yet again, said, "*You'll never know if you keep procrastinating, Lad. Let's get going.*"

Rising from where he knelt, the Guardsman stumbled as the Dragon King with whom he shared his soul knocked him on the back of the knees with a slap of Magic. "*One day, I'm gonna figure out how to get even with you for all the years of abuse.*"

"*I welcome the challenge.*"

Not bothering to comment because it just would've led to a long, drawn-out word battle Cass didn't have the brain power to engage in at the moment, he straightened the tawny Stetson atop his head, turned to the left and headed toward the footbridge that was always so beautifully decorated with flowers for every season. It didn't matter that he hadn't been back to the Chihuahuan Desert in years. The delicately painted blossoms were something he could always count on being there.

Over the years, he'd asked the name of the artist, but no one had ever answered. He didn't know if the artist wanted to stay anonymous, or if those he'd asked simply didn't have the answer. Either way, he hoped to one day meet that person and thank them for adding a little sunshine to every trip he made to the canyon.

Inhaling deeply, knowing how close he was to not only Chief Cheveyo but, by all accounts, his Mate, Cass, blew out the breath. Turning back yet again, he watched a swarm of Dragonflies fluttering amongst the multitude of blossoms and prayed that his Mate would love this place, his home, as much as he did. It was where he wanted to settle down, where he wanted to raise his kids, where he wanted to spend his happily ever after.

One last look and yet another Magical prod from his Dragon King, and Cass turned toward the Res. Smiling at the painted flowers, he inhaled deeply and then exhaled, pushing all the tension and trepidation from his body.

Reaching for the wooden handrail, he whispered, "For better or for worse, let's get this show on the road."

Brushing the handrail with the tips of his fingers, an electrical current shot from the well-worn white oak into his hand. Racing up his arm, it supercharged his heart, did a loopty loop up through his brain, danced around his lungs then splashed down in the depths of his soul like the shuttle hitting the jetty at Cape Canaveral.

Driven to his knees by the sheer magnitude and strength of the memories, his mind was swamped with sights and sounds and images that he knew beyond all shadow of a doubt were not his own. Looking through the eyes of another, he saw people and places he knew so well.

Aunt Barb, Uncle Owen, all of his cousins, the Sampson Twins, and even Cheveyo and Momma Maybelle were there. He felt himself swooping through the air and instantly knew that he was on the tire swing outside the Chief's house on Sequoyah Hill. The long red curls that glistened in the sunlight had to be that of a little girl, and the giggles that felt as if they were coming from his own lips were most assuredly female.

Then, in an instant, the perspective changed. No longer was he in the mind of the person whose memories he was experiencing, but he was watching as if the recollections were a movie.

Absolutely the cutest little girl he'd ever seen, with bright red curls in ponytails tied with blue ribbons, was playing with another older girl in Momma Maybelle's back-yard. With her hands cupped on either side of her face, her sparkling green eyes twinkled with mischief as she looked at the bark of the Sugar Maple tree and counted to ten. "Ready or not, Augie! Here I come!" She shouted before taking off as fast as her little legs would carry her.

Before she found her playmate, the scene once again changed. No longer was she a little girl, and sadly, neither was she smiling.

Sadness poured off her like raindrops off a duck's back as she stood beside a funeral pyre. Tears streamed down her face as two bodies wrapped in the ceremonial cloths, one adorned with the Timber Wolf head medallion of the Thorntree Pack and the other wearing one with an insignia Cass didn't understand, but the owner of the memories knew all too well.

Her thoughts were jumbled, her sorrow almost unbearable, but still, at such a young age, she spoke with the wisdom of the Ancients. Her voice was music to his years. He wanted to go back in time and take away all the pain of losing those she loved so dearly.

"Today, under the moon and stars, I ask the Great Creator, the Universe, and The Powers That Be to welcome my momma and daddy home. Their time here on this Earth was short, and I-I w-w-ish..."

Unable to go on, Cheveyo took over, and that memory ended. It had been her parents. There was no doubt. And he knew they died an honorable death on the battlefield, protecting those they loved–doing everything in their power to make sure that very special little girl had the best life possible.

"Just like my mom and dad," he whispered.

From one beat of his heart to the next, the movie of his Mate's life–for that's who she was, of that there could be no doubt–started again. Flashes of important events, birthdays, holidays, and celebrations at the Res all zoomed by in a blur that only his Enchanted eyesight could decipher. Not everything he saw was happy. The woman made for him by the Universe had experienced her share of ups and downs. She'd fought hard to become an award-winning photographer, with her pictures in more publications all over the world than Cass knew existed.

His Mate was fantastic. Her intelligence was woven into the very fabric of her being. It shone around her, a bright, warm, and wonderful light that called to his soul. Cass was drawn to her like a moth to a flame. He wanted to be nowhere but by her side.

From her memories, he knew that she was incredibly talented, seeing things in animals, people, and nature as no other ever had. She was his complement, the other half of his soul. She was everything he'd ever wanted–*ever needed*.

And her beauty was beyond compare. Flaming red hair, highlighted with hues of golden honey, fresh pumpkin, and chestnut, perfectly matched Blár's fire and magnificently enhanced her flawless ivory skin, blush cheeks, and brilliant Emerald eyes.

Not to mention the spattering of freckles dancing across her nose and the apples of her cheeks–he dreamt of worshipping each one with adoring kisses as he marked with his scent for the world to know that she was his Mate, the woman made for Caspian MacAllen by the Universe and no other.

"She. Is. Mine."

The longer he gazed into her memories and took in all she was, the deeper he fell in love with this glorious woman, and he didn't even know her name. The Mating Bond in the center of his soul burned brighter than the sun. Blár was roaring at the top of his lungs and pawing at every corner of Cass's mind.

Both man and Dragon King knew this woman was the other half of their soul. She was the Light to their Darkness. She was their Hope.

No sooner had the thought passed between them than did the flashes of recollections come to a screeching halt. Disoriented for the briefest of seconds, he slammed his eyes shut. Waiting less than a second, he opened them wide, and his heart stopped cold.

Through a veil of Ancient Mysticism, he could see the woman made for him by the Universe and she was quite literally the most gorgeous woman he'd ever laid eyes on. Unfortunately, she was smack dab in the middle of a shitstorm of epic proportions. Standing five feet tall, if she was an inch and still sporting a flowing mane of long, red curls, his Mate was brandishing an ornate Cherokee War Club like it was what she was born to do.

There was no fear. There was no trepidation. There was only the knowledge that her fight was just and right, and it was what she had to do to save her people.

Eyes flying to her assailant, Cass couldn't believe his eyes. He'd only ever seen anything like the rider on the Dead Horse in pictures–and they did not come close to the pure menace, malice, and destruction rolling off the Evil Earth Spirit known as the Uya.

Before he could think, come up with a plan, or yell for his Mate to get out of the way, she literally taunted the Uya, yelling, "You came here for me, Bitch. So, let's do this!"

The Evil Earth Spirit's retort was instantaneous and earsplitting as she bellowed, "I will have you, Abigail Annabella Addams. I will drink the blood from your veins. I will grind your bones to dust. I will wear your teeth around my neck as a warning to all who dare oppose me. Your defeat will fan the flames of my Reign. You will die knowing that your loss is that of the world, of all that is Good... of the Light." Her hiss echoed, riding the airwaves in a dissonant chord that made the hairs at the nape of Cass's neck stand on end–and she wasn't done.

"But before that, Abigail Annabella Addams, the first True and Natural Nûññë'hï Warrior to walk the Earth in many years, I will take all you hold dear. I will bend and warp and kill your friend, your family, and most importantly, your Uktena. Today is the day of your death. Today is the death of the Everlasting Hope!"

"Hold on, Mo stór! I'm coming! From this day forward, we fight side by side!" Cass roared directly into Abigail's mind.

Jumping to his feet, Cass summoned the Magic of the

Ancient Dragons and called to the Dragon King with whom he shared his soul, *"Time to do what we do, Old Man. Pour on the..."*

And that was as far as he got before Blár took control of not only the Guardsman's body but his mind and the immense amount of magnanimous Ancient Mysticism, Enchantment, and unwavering Blessing flooding into every fiber of his being. Thanking the Heavens that his Dragon King was controlling the whirl of manic rage and the unrelenting need to rid the world of the Evil Earth Spirit who dared to challenge the woman made for him by the Universe, Cass's head was thrown back as far as it would go, and glorious flames flew from his lips as he roared his supremacy for all to hear.

The racing of paws, hooves, and all manner of feet hit the ground in wild abandon, and the inhabitants of McKittrick Canyon sought cover. Although fear rode the airwaves, none of them went far. Peeking their heads around stumps, through leaves, from under bushes, and out of burrows, they all wanted to behold the majesty of the coming of a true Dragon King.

Seizures, tremors, and all manner of convulsions shook his body. His blood ran cold. Then it flipped to boiling. Then it returned to freezing. Over and over, shivers wracked every cell of his body and then sweat ran like rivers over every inch of his flesh, switching back and forth in the blink of an eye. Contracting and contorting, his very physique prepared for the transformation from man to mighty Dragon King.

In an instant, both agreed that they needed the mobility of the compact, indestructible form of Warrior Dragon. The Magic of the Ancient Dragon Kings, the Original Mage, and of the Knights whose souls were shared with the original

Dragons beat against Cass's body with the force of a jackhammer destroying concrete.

Forcing the large, elongated muscles he would have used for flying had they been Shifting in their Winged Warrior into his chest, biceps, and quads, his torso expanded in width and breadth at an unparalleled rate. It was obvious Blár was rushing the Shift as never before to join their Mate in battle, and Cass was there for it all.

The thick grass, sandy soil, and roots of plants and trees beneath his feet shuddered and shook. The small pebbles and flat rocks of the creek's edge danced along the terrain as the long claws jutting from his toes dug deep, providing the Dragon King with much-needed stability as his body grew into the unstoppable Warrior it was meant to be.

An inferno, the flaming shards of silver and blazing spikes of iron bore for battle by the Irish God of War, Neith, sliced through the flesh and bone of his back. Every inch of his body had to be torn asunder and then reconstructed into the unbeatable Ancient Warrior they were destined to be.

Cartlidge and bone stretched, joints and tendons popped to create what would have been wings. At half their normal length, the tips snapped downward, curling toward the ground in the blink of an eye.

No sooner had one reconstruction occurred than another began. As the pointed finger claws were just about to touch the blades of grass, they twisted upward and shot toward his shoulder blades. Pushing through the thick layer of crystalline blue scales, they ripped through every layer of his body as if it were no more than wet paper.

Bones continued to shatter, and muscles unrelentingly tore with extreme precision and meticulous accuracy until the Dragon King no longer possessed wings at all. Instead, he had what looked like huge, semi-circular blades of an oversized Leviathan Kratos Axe jutting from his back with long, venomous finger-claws extending from the razor-sharp edges.

Moving them up and down and forward and back, he felt the acidic poison to which there was no antidote flowing through the capillaries, racing to the ready should their assistance be needed. To kill an enemy with venom created by the Morrigan, the Queen of Nightmares, the Celtic Goddess of War, Death, and Fate, was a last resort. Blár thought it too easy. He preferred a fair fight between combatants, but when it came down to the life of the opposition or that of their Mate. He would strike with wild abandon and walk away as the enemy died a horrible, agonizing death.

Raising his hands, he watched the flesh at the ends of his fingers peel away and talons jut from within. As soon as they saw the light of day, the barbed daggers made of bone doubled in size and girth. Their hooked tips tingled with the need to rip through any and all who dared to stand between him and the woman made for them but the Universe.

In a matter of mere seconds, he stood ten feet tall, a mountain of muscle, Magic, and incomparable rage, Blár raised his hands, snapped his fingers, and walked through the portal swirling of the Magic of their Elders before him. Watching through the eyes of his Dragon King, Cass gasped as, a second later, they exited the vortex to find devastation everywhere he looked.

The trees were bare, their trucks black with decay and rot. Dead leaves, plants, and flowers littered the ground, along with decaying fruit, moldy vegetables, and decomposing flesh of small game animals.

But it was the burning, smoldering Christmas decorations strewn about and defiled with hatred and rage that shot a dagger through his heart. Then, the suffering, the agony, and the sorrow of illness and death attacked his senses like a heat-seeking missile

The Uya, the Evil Earth Spirit was attacking everything right and good in the Thorntree Reservation. It was seeking to destroy the center of not only the Spirit of the Great Cherokee Tribe, but also of the tenacious Timber Wolf, Laignech Fáelad of Pack Fianna, the Alpha who shares his soul with none other than the Great Chief Cheveyo.

Following the Mating Bond, Blár raced across yards, through gardens, and over gates to reach Abigail as Cass opened the unique mental connection they shared with the Chief and shouted, *"Cheveyo! Cheveyo, where are you? Are you okay? Your people..."*

"He's gone!" Came the sharp, two-word replay from his Mate. Her voice was music to his ears, no matter the situation. She was simply fantastic. His heart was full to bursting and he still had not seen her with his own eyes.

Then she added, *"Are you comin'? I gotta bitch ridin' the skeleton of a horse who wants to kick my ass and I think she needs a lesson in manners!"* And he officially fell head over heels in love.

With a wave of his massive paw, the granite and basalt wall at the back right corner of the ranch-style home disappeared. The scene before them was something out of the Superhero movie, or one of the graphic novels he'd seen Jay MacLendon and the O'Brien twins reading and watching during his short time at the Golden Fire Clan.

Most of the room was filled with the woman, Sydney Kavanaugh, he'd met at Rayne and Kyndel's, and a woman he instantly recognized as Auggie Addams. The blond was frantically pulling copious amounts of Healing Magic from the core of the Earth while the Timber She-Wolf's breathing was dangerously shallow and her heartbeat perilously slow. Cass could only pray that Syd could keep Auggie alive while he and Abbie sought to destroy the Evil Earth Spirit.

In the far corner, locked inside a corroded, slimy ball of Sorcery and Black Magic, stood Abbie, poised for the fight of her life with the ceremonial War Club at the ready. Determination was written all over her face. Fire burned white hot in the depths of her Emerald eyes. Her heart beat with the conviction of a True and Natural Nûññë'hï Warrior. It was time to join forces with the woman it felt as if he'd loved since the beginning of time and destroy the Uya.

"*No, Lad,*" Blár objected. "*We will not be destroying her. We will...*"

"*We will be sending her back where she came from,*" Cass cut off the Dragon King, mimicking his thick Highlands brogue as he continued. "*Because we will not, nor can we, destroy anything of the Darkness. It serves an essential purpose for those things springing from the Abyss to continue to exist. They do not have to thrive. They simply must survive. For without them, we would not know Light. Without the Bad, we would not know the Good. Without...*"

"*Aye, Lad,*" Blár sighed. "*I see you might actually have been listening for all these decades, nay centuries.*"

"Yeah, I heard, and I understand, but I don't have to like it. Look at that poor woman in the bed. Feel all the pain and suffering this single Evil Earth Spirit is causing. She doesn't deserve to..."

Then it clicked. Cass remembered everything. Abigail, Abbie as she'd been called then. She was Auggie's little cousin, the carrot-topped child with more freckles than face who'd followed behind them, asking a million questions and begging to follow them into whatever mischief lay ahead.

Cheveyo had been right. Aunt Barbara knew the truth. He had met his Mate many years earlier.

And now the stars had aligned, and they would be together.

"Only if you get your ass over here before this bitch charges at me!" Abbie snapped. *"More of that 'let's fight together. Whacha' say, Dragon Man?"*

He could feel her patience wearing thin. His Mate did not suffer fools, and she most assuredly did not like to wait for anything.

The Dead Horse's hooves pawed the ground. It lifted its head. Its eyes, a glowing amber that strengthened with every passing second, speared Abbie with a look of unrelenting hatred. Squealing, almost like a pig in distress, *the Deid Cuddie* flared its nostrils, snorted furiously, and blew black soot and steam in every direction.

There was no time to lose. Cass not only needed to help his Mate send the Uya back to where she came from, mark her as his own, and have an amazing Mating Ceremony they would remember forever, but he also needed to be by her side—no matter the situation. Wherever Abbie was, he would be there too, for the rest of forever.

Without another thought, they burst through the bewitched wall of Black Magic into the microcosm of wickedness and malice. As soon as the soles of Blár's giant feet hit the ground, he extended his arm and reached into the Ether of the Earth. Wrapping his fingers around a thick leather grip, the side of his hand was flush against the gemstone pommel as he pulled the long, wide-bladed dagger, the Jeweled Scian of Maeve, the Irish Goddess of the Dragons and the Land, into his reality. Glittering with light blue gems and snow-white diamonds that perfectly matched the scales of his Dragon King, the Guardsman held it tightly within his left hand as he moved closer to his Mate.

With his right elbow slightly behind Abbie's shoulder, he whispered into her mind, *"Do you trust me?"*

"Do I have a choice?"

"Always."

"Right answer, Flyboy. I trust you with the life of our Tribe."

Cass's heart skipped a beat. Her words meant the world to him. She recognized exactly who he was—not only her Mate but also of the Thorntree Tribe. It was a given that she trusted him. If she hadn't, there was no doubt she would've beaten the living crap out of him with her War Club when he appeared in the crazy sphere of madness created by the Uya.

Regardless of what *could* have happened, he'd never had a doubt. He knew her, and she knew him. It was the way it was meant to be. They'd been made for each other. The instant he touched her mind, he saw her memories, and she saw his.

He'd felt the strength of the Mating Bond growing stronger the closer he got to her. Their souls had already started to become one. Their hearts beat in sync. The connection that could only be shared by True Fated Mates was alive, well, and unstoppable within them both.

But the fact that she believed in him and knew he would do everything in his power to protect and save the people they both held dear was more than he could have ever hoped for. And he would *not* let her down.

"Thank you, Mo chridhe. I will not fail."

"I believe you, Loverboy. Now, less words, more action."

Letting the plan flow from his mind to hers, he felt her recognition at precisely the same moment that the *Deid Cuddie* charged. Doing exactly as he'd asked, Abbie let go of the War Club with her left hand and swung it wide. He slid the right arm of their Warrior Dragon around her waist and hooked the paw around the perfect curve of her hip.

Moving as if they'd done the move a hundred times, Abbie bent her knees as the Dragon lifted her off the ground. Throwing her into the air and over their shoulder in one fluid motion, neither Guardsman nor Dragon King breathed until her legs slipped over the tops of their shoulders and her feet hooked under their arms.

"Hold on, Hot Stuff," Cass shouted into her mind. *"Takin' you for a spin."*

"I thought you'd never ask."

Stepping to the left, the Dragon King leaned into the movement, tucked his chin, and spun with pure adrenalin, the love of his Mate, and the Magic of the Universe. Raising his left hand, the one holding the Scian of Maeve, as high as he could, he trusted Abbie to follow the plan, to go low with the War Club she held in her right.

Feeling the heat from the fire of the Underworld powering the Dead Horse the closer it and the Uya came, those unholy flames thrashed at the impenetrable crystalline scales covering his body in an attempt to reach his neck. "She thinks to take our head, Lad. Have you ever heard something so foolhardy"

Unable to respond to his Dragoon King's levity in the face of an adversary from the Underworld, Cass's heart skipped a beat as he roared, *"Abbie has no protection!"*

"Never fear," Blár countered, unwavering calm confidence flowing from Dragon King to man. *"Our Mate is dressed for battle. Of that, you can be sure."*

A picture of Abbie instantly appeared in his mind, and damn if it wasn't magnificent. Head held high, hair flowing behind her like the flames from the Great Goddess Herself, she sat upon the back of the Warrior Dragon as the one True and Natural Nûññë'hï she was meant to be–and she wore the crystalline blue scales of the Dragons of the Clan of the Goddess Maeve. With a chest plate of Dragon scales, matching gauntlets covering her arms from wrist to elbow, and a face shield resembling a mask, she was more than combat ready.

"I love a good fashion show as much as the rest, but we have exactly two–point–two seconds until..."

"Shut up, Faye! We're workin' here!"

Appreciating the banter between Abbie and the Timber She-Wolf with whom she, at least partially, shared her soul, Cass couldn't help but agree with his Mate. And not a moment too soon.

Completing the first revolution at the perfect time, he swept the sharp edge of his blade with impeccable precision, *knowing* it would hit the mark. Slicing through its knees as if they were nothing more than hot butter, the bone-chilling screams of the Dead Horse were only topped by the shrieks coming from the Uya as the jagged and barbed points of the War Club slashed across the paper-thin flesh of her neck.

Flying through the air as the *Deid Cuddie* fell forward on what was left of its front legs, the Evil Earth Spirit hit the wall of her own Black Magic with the force of a speeding train. Sparks flew. The unmistakable sizzle of something being seared abraded his ears. The foul, acerbic stench of burnt and rotting flesh filled the air, reminiscent of the foul odor of singed hair mixed with toxic chemicals he'd experienced during the clean-up of the nuclear explosion at Chernobyl in the Ukraine. It had been horrible and something he'd unfortunately experienced many times throughout the centuries in many different situations.

However, in this case, he wanted more. He wanted the Uya to suffer and bleed for what she'd done to the Thorn-tree Tribe and wanted to do to his Mate. She had to be punished. No, he couldn't kill her, but he could bring her to the brink over and over again.

Continuing to turn, the Warrior Dragon slammed their massive right foot onto the ground when they were in the perfect position and came to a screeching halt. Watching and waiting, the Warrior Dragon's eyes never left the Uya. He could feel Abbie's impatience growing with every beat of their hearts. She wanted to stab the Evil Earth Spirit again and again straight through the heart. The bitch had dared to attack her Tribe, *their people*. She thought of nothing but shoving the dying body of the foulest Being ever created by the Darkness back into whatever Pit she'd crawled out of... But Cass also heard the thoughts of not only his Dragon King but of the Ditlihi and the Timber She-Wolf and knew they were all in agreement that before sending the Evil Earth Spirit back into the Darkness, they needed answers.

The Uya was a messenger and assassin of sorts. She never acted on her own. She was always doing someone's bidding.

But who? And where the hell was Cheveyo and Momma Maybelle?

More than ready when the Evil Earth Spirit gave up on the Dead Horse coming to her aide, he wasn't at all surprised when she pulled the Spear of Carman from the ether. Of course, the Black Sorceress who'd been cursed by the Tuatha De Danann and was sentenced to an eternity in the deepest Pit of the Underworld by the Dadga, had given the Uya her spear. Evil always begat evil.

Then, before Cass's shock had time to register, Abbie

yelled, "Oh, hell, no! I call foul! You can't pull out the big spear! We just got started! That's some bullshit right there!"

"Abbie, Mo ghràdh," Cass mentally whispered. *"Maybe don't..."*

"Arggghhhhh," the Uya shrieked.

Jumping to her feet, she held the Spear of Carman at arm's length in front of her chest. Her hands were perfectly placed, and her shoulders expertly bent. She was ready to whip that weapon in whatever way was needed to do maximum damage to her enemy.

Trying to look her in the eye, Cass was momentarily at a loss. The Uya had no eyes. Then he felt the vacuous pull of the Darkness, the Sorcery that kept the Evil Earth Spirit alive and kicking.

"Look up," Abbie snapped, her tone sharp and efficient, something he appreciated at the time.

Gaze darting upward, he sarcastically snorted, *"Thanks, M'eudail. Wonder how long it'll take for that image to leave my brain."*

"We'll just have to make better, happier ones to drive that ugliness away."

"I like the way you think."

"And I think you need to pay attention," Blár growled. *"Both of you."*

Knowing there was no use to answer back, Cass carefully took in the beady, black eyes of the slithering creatures hissing and spitting atop her head. They resembled snakes, but he could tell they were so much more.

Rearing up, striking at the air and expelling some caustic liquid that bubble and crackled as soon as the air hit it, they undulated and writhed atop her head. Heads snapping left then right they saw everything. Coiling then shooting upward and tightly twisting their bodies, they got a three-hundred-and-sixty-degree view of everything.

And that meant the Uya did, too.

"Those creepy snake things see for her," Abbie telepathically whispered. *"That's how she knows where we are."*

"And let us not forget, those bastardized versions of the inland taipan are incredibly poisonous," Blár added,

"Good to know," Abbie breathed, and at that moment, Cass knew she and his Dragon King were going to get along just fine. She had to be the first person in history not to want to say, 'duh' when Blár spit out one of his well-studied facts.

With his focus never wavering, the Guardsman recognized the constant motion and sliding from side to side the Uya was doing for exactly what it was—a tactic to close the space between them. Mirroring her movement, he could feel her frustration growing. She was in a hurry. She wanted them out of the way. She was...

Moving so fast she was nothing but a blur of black gore and translucent flesh, the Evil Earth Spirit shot from one side of the vile, infested bubble to the other. Holding perfectly still, only moving his eyes, Cass used the Dragon King's huge, elliptically pupiled orbs to watch what she was doing and anticipate what was coming next.

Over and over, she did the same thing. Again and again, she ranted and raved about what she would do to not only Cass and Abbie, but to Blár and the Ditlihi as soon as she had them incapacitated and in her domain.

Powered by pure rage and unadulterated malevolence, rancid green spittle and black flecks of bloody phlegm flew into the air with every word she spat, and then her threats turned really nasty. "Death is too good for the likes of you! I will suck the blood from your veins! I will feast on the marrow of your bones. I will feed your flesh to the *Deid*

Cuddie, and all the while, I will keep you alive. Your suffering will sustain me for centuries. You are nearly immortal, and I plan to use that to my advantage. Forever, I tell you. You will suffer forever! And the world you love so much, the people you care for with all your worthless hearts, oh, how they will suffer. The loss of the Everlasting Hope–of all Hope–will cripple the world, leaving it primed for me and mine. We will reign supreme! I will..."

BANG!

An unexpected, incandescent funnel cloud erupted to the right of the Evil Earth Spirit. A blinding, fluorescent lavender light devoured everything in its path.

The air roared. A deafening crackle speared his eardrums as a monstrous, guttural boom shook the foundation of the house. A wave of pure Energy, Light, and incredible Magic shattered the walls of the vile bubble. Gooey, gory shards were impaled into the walls. Plaster, wood, and pieces of rock and cement exploded into a thousand daggers, flinging deadly debris across the room.

A howl unlike anything Cass, Abbie, or even Blár and Faye had ever heard filled the room, expanding in every direction, growing louder and more profound until it was joined with another. The ground continued to shake, not from another explosion, but from the sheer magnitude and force yet another Magical presence was bringing to the party.

"What the fu...? Holy shi...!"

His expletives were cut off as gale force winds blew in from the North, South, East and West. From one second to the next, the devastation and debris was gone and at the four corners of the insidious bubble stood four of the largest Timber Wolves to ever walk the Earth.

Standing directly in front of the Uya with its left flank

just a few feet from the Warrior Dragon was the largest, the Leader, Laignech Fáelad. Five feet from shoulder to floor, the tip of his ears had to be seven feet tall. His paws were huge. From the end of his nose to the tip of his tail, the mighty Timer Wolf was eight feet long if he were an inch.

His chest was massive, like an NFL defensive lineman's, with a single stripe of thick, voluminous gray fur that matched the man, the Chief with whom the King of the Wolves of Ossory shared his soul. It was Cheveyo, and that meant the Lupine to the East was his son, Dasan, and to the West was the other, Elan. That left absolutely no doubt that standing at the South Watch Tower was none other than Momma Maybelle.

"Stay close, Isi," Cheveyo's voice whispered through Abbie's mind a split second before he added, *"Today is the day, Caspian. Today is the day we fight for those we've lost."*

Not waiting for even an entire beat of Cass and Abbie's hearts, or for either to respond, Cheveyo threw back his head and howled again. The sound, a call to arms, filled the very ether of the fabric of the universe. It shook the core of the All Powerful and called to the Great Creator for strength.

And that was when all hell broke loose.

A well-oiled War Party, the Timber Wolves launched themselves into the air. It was magnificent to watch and heart stopping to witness. Unfortunately, the Uya was prepared.

Before the pads of the Timber Wolves front paws touched down, a shrill whistle sliced through the air, assaulting everything with ears for miles. In the next instant, a Horde of Skeenah appeared out of thin air. They stood, knelt, creeped and crawled in a circle around all involved.

Abominations, mismatched and animated creatures

from the depths of the Underworld, the Skeenah, the ones both Cass and his Mate had seen take the lives of their parents, were at least four deep and shoulder to shoulder. They had come to kill, to devour, to massacre everything Good and decimate the Light.

The stench of sulfur, brimstone, and utterly despicable Black Magic permeated the air. Thick, black fog wafted and slithered, snaking its way toward the Dragon King, Abbie, and the Timber Wolves with intent so nefarious that the scales on the back of Blár's Warrior Dragon tingled.

There was no preamble, no postering, no more games, before the Warrior Dragon could draw a breath, the Uya raised the Spear of Carman and the Skeenah attacked. They were everywhere. Grotesque and lumbering, they were faster than they looked, and hellbent on leaving a trail of death and destruction in their path...

But Cass and Blár were having none of it.

Racing straight for the Uya, who stood at the center of the fight, the Warrior Dragon slashed and hacked with expert precision with the Blade of Maeve. Spinning left and right, going high, then dropping to his knees, the enemies that didn't meet their demise at the end of his sword were either beaten by his Mate or incinerated by the flames of Dragon Fire he expelled at will.

The fight was so tense, so full of aggression, agitation, and horror that it seemed to go one forever while actually happening in the blink of an eye. The Evil Earth Spirit was wily, avoiding his attack and that of the Timber Wolves at every turn.

"Go left!" Abbie screamed, her arm flying out past the Warrior Dragon's ear as she pointed to the spot where Cheveyo, Elan, Dasan, and Momma Maybelle were moving in on the Uya.

Mowing down the adversaries with uninhibited fervor, he left a trail of bloody and charred remains in his path. With only three feet to go, The Evil Earth Spirit was so close he could feel the heat of the Fire of Hell on his scales. Then, his Mate shrieked as the welcome weight of her body on his shoulders was lifted away.

Spinning to the left and to the right, he looked everywhere. Then, an extraordinary light called his attention upward, and the sight he beheld was simply astonishing. He couldn't believe his eyes. He wouldn't have believed it if he wasn't watching the miracle unfold in real-time.

Levitating high above the combatants with her head thrown back, her arms spread wide, and the illumination of the Heavens glowing like a halo around her entire body was none other than the woman made for him by the Universe, his Mate, the reason his heart took its next beat. Ready to call out to her, to tell her how he felt, the light turned into something more... something magnificent... something... something...

"It is the Light of the Great Creator," Cheveyo's voice whispered into Cass's mind. *"She is becoming. Abbie is becoming all she was ever meant to be. You have done it, Caspian. You have returned the True and Natural Nûññë'hï to us."*

He had absolutely no clue what the old Chief was going on about, but one thing was for sure, his Mate's transformation had stopped everyone dead in their tracks–especially the Uya and her Skeenah Horde...

And she wasn't done yet.

White Fire, the legendary flames of the Goddess of Maeve, flew from her chest. Filling the air with brilliant illumination, the blazing plumes wove and danced in every direction. Totally captivated by the light show, Cass didn't know anything else was happening until the raucous howls and agonizing wails ripped through the beauty of the moment.

For what seemed like the hundredth time, the Warrior Dragon was spinning in one direction and then the other. Just like dominoes falling in some intricate formation, the Skeenah horde fell to the floor. Gasping and hacking, their caustic, black blood spewed in every direction before they gasped. A collective death rattle echoed throughout the room, and they lay dead.

A shrill, unholy shriek ripped the resulting silence as the Evil Earth Spirit raised the Spear of Carman over her head. "Die Nûñnë'hï! To Hell with all you are and all you represent! Death to the Everlasting..."

But that was as far as she got.

Stopping as if she was frozen, standing exactly where she'd been with her mouth open wide, the snakes upon her head in suspended animation and oily black gunk flowing down her chin, the Uya was stuck. Unsure what was happening, the Warrior Dragon's gaze snapped to Abbie as she floated to the ground.

Then he looked at Cheveyo.

Then to the other three Timber Wolves.

Everyone wore the same expression of extreme shock and utter surprise.

Eyes flying back to the Evil Earth Spirit, Cass gasped, *"Holy shit! Look at her chest!"*

And there it was–a long golden arrow with flames of the same hue burning their way through the Uya's chest. Unable to move, still alive and caught in the snare of something or someone, she was slowly becoming ash right before his eyes.

As she fell to her knees, the Warrior Dragon saw who had shoved that arrow through the Evil Earth Spirit's heart.

He barked with laughter as Abbie snorted, "Well, hell, Syd, how about that fancy shootin'?"

"Just trying to keep up with you."

"Y-you w-will not w-win," the Uya gasped, her chest rattling with the last vestiges of her earthly form. "The M-Master w-will... H-he w-will... H-H..."

Before she could even finish her threat, she took her last breath on the planet.

Taking a single step toward his Mate, the Warrior Dragon opened his mouth to profess his love, but nothing came. Blown away by a huge gust of wind, not only his words were gone, but also was the remains of the Uya and her Skeenah Horde.

Waiting, counting to three, he only moved when he was sure nothing was going to happen. Making it halfway across the area that separated them, Blár retreated to the background of their shared psyche, leaving Cass back in human form to catch his Mate as she launched herself into his arms.

Raining kisses all over his face, she whispered into his mind, *"Well, hello, Caspian MacAllen. Nice to finally properly meet you. Wanna get hitched?"*

7

"Thank the Heavens Auggie and everybody else are okay?"

"You can say that again."

"And that everything went back to normal as soon as She Who Will Not Be Named went back to whatever rock in the corner of the Underworld she crawled out of."

"Amen! But I still can't figure out why Cheveyo and Momma Maybelle have no memory of where they were before Dasan and Elan found them."

"Me neither."

"Well, I guess it's a puzzle for another day."

"Have I said thank you yet?"

"Only about a hundred times," Syd chuckled. "And just like I said all of those times, it was my pleasure."

"Did you know you could do that?"

"The flaming arrow or the whole 'Dragon in my head' thing?"

"Well, both," Abbie snickered.

"Shavon told me that my birth parents were human but

from the Original Mage's bloodline. She and the other Oracles showed me where to find everything that had ever been written about it–me–and we were all pretty sure I would at least have some Ancient Dragon Magic and maybe some of their abilities, but I never imagined..."

"Dude, are you gonna be able to Shift?"

"No clue."

"And the flaming arrow?"

"Well, the best I can figure is that I am somehow related to the Celtic Goddess Maeve, and that means..."

"That means we're really sisters now!" Abbie squealed. Jumping up from her dressing table, she crossed the room as fast as she could and wrapped her best friend up in a big hug.

Feeling like the last piece had fallen into place, the redhead loosened her arms and stepped back. "Well, I mean sisters by marriage and a little removed because..."

"Because the Dragon King who shares his soul with your hunka–hunka–burnin' love is the only remaining Winged Warrior from the Clan of the Goddess Maeve?"

"See? You know me so well."

Gently bopping the tip of her nose, Sydney giggled, "Just remember, we have been sisters of the heart since the first moment we met."

"I could never forget."

Waving her hand in the air, Syd tried to pretend to be irritated as she arched her right eyebrow and shooed, "Now, get your happy heiney back over to that dressing table and let me finish your hair. You don't want to keep that sexy Mate of yours waiting any longer than you have to."

"You are so right." Hurrying back across the room, Abbie sat down as Sydney grabbed the brush from the table and attempted to tame her unruly curls. "Just pull and tug all you have to. Since my 'Becoming,' as Cheveyo and Momma Maybelle keep calling it, my hair has been damn near untamable."

"Do you know why?"

"Nope, but I bet you do."

"Let's just say I think I do."

"So, spill."

Watching a million thoughts pass through Sydney's expressive blue eyes, Abbie waited, praying for a few answers. Thankfully, the wait wasn't long as the blond nodded and began. "So, I told you that for the last ten years Shavon and the Oracles have pretty much had me researching anything and everything about my heritage, the Dragons, and any other phenomena the Earth hasn't seen in centuries."

"Yep, I remember," Abbie concurred. "That's how we met. Down in the basement of the old library in Dallas."

"Absolutely."

"Those archives were so dusty and disorganized. Thank the Heavens you were there before I got trapped under an avalanche of books that weighed almost as much as me."

"For real, that whole 'there are no coincidences' always seems to come into play, doesn't it?"

"Damn sure does," Abbie chuckled. "Now, get on with it. I want to hear this story."

"Okay," Syd laughed. "You are always so impatient."

"Yeah, well, this time I actually have a reason," Pointing to her neck, she winked, "I gots to have that Mating Mark, or I'm gonna be an invisible member of the People Who Will Live Forever, and that is not something I want to be."

"Girl, you are not gonna be invisible. You have already

'Become.' The Mating Mark and the... ahem... consumma-tion..." She waggled her eyebrows. "...are just formalities."

"Formalities are exactly what I need," Abbie stressed the last word, pretended to swoon, and then laughed so hard Syd had to stop brushing her hair.

"Oh, stop, Girl, You're gonna make me blush."

As soon as she could breathe again, she motioned with her hand and promised, "Okay, okay, I'll behave. Tell me what you know."

"Okay, so I read about the People Who Would Live Forever and the One True and Natural Nûñnë'hï Warrior, and that brought up a lot of questions. So, I called Momma Maybelle, and she referred me to..."

"...Emma Evilhawk and the Sisters of Wisdom."

"Girl, you are too smart for your own good sometimes."

"Nope, just in awe. I thought about going to their Reser-vation, but honestly, I was scared of what they would tell me." She inhaled, exhaled, and then whispered, "Is it true that with one look, they know everything about you?"

"Yep, and a lot more."

"A lot more?"

"For sure," Sydney nodded, her eyes wide. "Emma met me at the gate, and before I could say hello, she told me all about my parents, why I had to go to the Citadel, and well... more shit that I ever thought I wanted to know."

"Damn."

"Yep, and I promise to share it all, but right now, I'll tell you what she told me about the True and Natural Nûñnë'hï Warrior and how I know you are the best–*the only* person for the job."

"Dude, if you make me cry and my mascara runs, I will make you tell Cass and Cheveyo why I'm late for the Mating Ceremony."

"Oh, hush," Syd chuckled. "I'm not goin' into detail. We're both criers and now is not the time."

"Thank the Heavens."

Snorting with laughter, Syd started to French braid Abbie's hair as she explained, "Okay, so I know you know that the whole Nûññë'hï thing is hereditary and matrilineal."

"Yep."

"And that's why you still share your soul with Faye, but you're not a Shifter."

"I do."

"Well, there is a part that is so you. I swear the writer knew you when they wrote, "The next True and Natural Nûññë'hï will be pure of heart. She will love and protect those she recognizes as Family with all that she is and protect them with her life. She will nurture the Spirit of Nature in all its forms. And she will know the man the Universe made for her with her heart and soul before her eyes behold him."

She was speechless. Abbie simply didn't know what to say. It did sound like her—even if it was a little flowery and verbose for her tastes.

"Then, when I talked to Emma, she went further. She explained the Everlasting Hope, the union of you and your Dragon, and that's when I knew the Universe really does not make mistakes. You were meant to be the True and Natural Nûññë'hï Warrior, and you and Cass are the Everlasting Hope. With y'all in the world, the good guys have the best chance of keeping the baddies at bay."

"Well, shit," Abbie sighed. Then smiling, she winked, "I can tell there's more, but I'm guessin' you either don't have time to tell me, it'll make me cry, or you're still lookin' for answers."

"Right on all three accounts," Syd nodded. "But I promise I won't stop until I have the answers."

"But first, you're gonna find your hunka-hunka-burnin' Dragon love, make him all better, and get hitched, right?"

"I am." Smiling, Syd fastened the bottom of Abbie's braid with the pearl barrette that had been her momma's. Then she added, "And I'm gonna find out who the Master is that the Uya was talkin' about, too."

"Just another reason I love you."

"Well, good." Patting her on the shoulder, Sydney kept going," Now, let's get you in your momma's gown and out there to that garden before Cass comes up here and hauls you out over his shoulder."

"He would do it, too."

Laughing as she slid the white lace dress over her head, Abbie looked at herself in the mirror as Sydney snapped the pearls lining her spine. Remembering what the photos of her mom looked like in the old-fashioned prairie style gown, the tips of her fingers brushed the intricately embroidered flames of light blue Barbara MacAllen and her cousin, Auggie had added to the square neckline.

The bodice fit perfectly and showed off her ample breasts that she knew from recent experience her Mate appreciated more than a little. Her cheeks heated with a blush as her hand swept over the slightly flared skirt where it sat on her curvy hip, and she remembered Cass saying, "Don't you dare lose a pound, *Mo ghràdh*. I love each and every one of your amazing curves and plan to properly worship them as soon as we are officially mated, and there's no danger of you becoming invisible."

"Ya' know I can hear your thoughts, right?" Syd giggled. "Not that I mind, but I thought I should remind you to practice shielding unless you want the Chief to get all the details.'

"Oh, shit," Abbie snorted. "That would not be good."

"But it would be funny."

"Yeah, it damn sure would."

Laughing with her best friend as she slid her feet into the white moccasins Momma Maybelle had made for her on her eighteenth birthday, Abbie took a final look in the mirror just as the clock in the hallway chimed eleven.

"Time to get this show on the road." Giving Syd a hug, she leaned back and reassured, "Sorry you can't be here for this one, but you better be back for the Dragon Ceremony in January."

"Oh, I will," the blond assured. "Right now, I'm gonna try to get back to Mom, Dad, and Baby Orla while it's still Christmas Eve."

"You can do it." Winking, Abbie added, "It'll be the best gift in the world."

Giving her a final hug and a kiss on the cheek, Sydney stepped back and smiled. "Now, go get hitched, and I'll see you in the new year."

"Thank you for everything, Syd," Abbie beamed. "I love you, Sis."

"I love you, too." And with that, she shimmered out of sight.

Turning towards the door, Abbie put one hand on the knob and the other on her momma's necklace. As always, the silver Triqueta– a triangular symbol made of three over-lapping arcs resembling a three-cornered knot–enclosed in a golden circle engraved with the words *Hope is the belief that anything is possible*, felt warm to the touch and filled her with love.

Opening the door, she looked over her shoulder one last

time and whispered, "I'm leaving this room a single woman and coming back with the love of my life. Sometimes, things really do work out."

Across the threshold and down the hall, she was outside and flashing to Momma Maybelle's garden in less than two seconds. Reappearing outside the gate, she shifted from one foot to the other repeating the words, *"Just breathe. Just breathe. Just breathe."*

Lost in thought, she almost jumped out of her skin when a warm hand touched her shoulder. Spinning to the right, she was overjoyed by Jed Thorntree's quick reflexes, which kept her from hitting the ground.

"Oh, shit, I am so sorry," he gasped. "You okay?"

"Yep, I'm good," she chuckled nervously. "Just lost in thought."

"I bet you are." Grinning, he handed the long-stemmed red roses she hadn't seen in his other arm until that very moment. "These are from Cass." Chuckling, he added with a wink, "But I bet you guessed that."

"I did," she snickered. "Unless there's something you need to tell me."

"No, ma'am, just that there's a note, and I'm gonna walk you down the aisle."

"Oh, I thought it was just gonna be Cass, me and Cheveyo."

"It is," the Stallion Shifter nodded. "I'm just getting' you where you need to be."

"Gotcha."

Pulling the small, ivory envelope from the center of the bouquet, Abbie's eyes filled with tears as she read Cass's words. *Today, we become one as it was always meant to be. They say we're the Everlasting Hope, but you, my dear Abbie, are my everything. All my love forever, C.*

Inhaling deeply, just barely keeping the happy tears from flowing, she turned back to Jed and nodded when he asked, "You ready to go, kiddo?"

"I was born ready."

"That you were, Abbie, my girl. That you were."

Slipping on the light blue shawl over her shoulders, also from her mom, she wrapped her arm around his. Giving a single nod, she stood perfectly still until Cheveyo walked to the center of the garden and stood in front of the fountain. Dressed in the original ceremonial clothing of the Cherokee, his long dark hair was pulled back in a thick braid that hung down the middle of his back. Shining in the light of the Yuletide Full Moon, the single grey chunk was front and center and the only hint of the Chief's age.

With her heart ready to pound out of her chest, Abbie was sure she was about to pass out, and then he appeared. Striding from the opposite side of the garden, he looked like a Knight from the Round Table and Prince Charming all rolled into one.

In a surcoat the exact hue of King Blár's scales, tight black pants, and black boots that shined like a diamond, he was everything she could have ever wanted in a Mate and so much more. His brown curls had just barely been tamed, and he'd left the sexy stubble around his mouth, on his chin, and lining his jaw just as she'd asked. Caspian Thomas MacAllen was drop-dead sexy, and he was all hers.

She watched as he placed the light blue woven blanket over his shoulders, loving the way the well-defined muscles of his arms and chest pushed against the fabric of the shirt under his surcoat. Catching his gaze, she couldn't help but mouth, *"You look damn good, Mr. Dragon Man."* Then, chuckling when he responded by whispering into her mind, *"Not as good as you, Mo stór."*

Walking in step with Jed, Abbie felt as if she was floating on air. She was headed towards her happily-ever-after and never wanted it to end.

Stopping just short of jumping into Cass's arms, she let Jed take the roses and reached for her Mate's hand as he reached for hers. Closing the distance, she pushed on her toes and tenderly placed a kiss on his cheek. Loving the feel of his smile against her lips, she whispered directly into his mind, *"Merry Christmas Eve, Hot Stuff."*

"Happy Birthday, Gorgeous."

Before she could answer, Cheveyo cleared his throat and then chuckled, "You kids know the quicker we make everything official, the sooner you get to be alone, right?"

"We do," they answered in unison, both laughing at the other.

"Okay then," the Chief chuckled. "Since y'all wanted to keep this ceremony small and intimate, I'll skip with the welcome speech and get right down to business. Let us pray."

Waiting until they'd bowed their heads, Cheveyo reverently began, "Now that you have found the one made for you by the Universe and the Great Creator, you will feel no rain, for you, Cass, and you, Abigail, will be shelter to each other. Neither will you feel cold, for each of you will be the warmth to the other. There will be no more loneliness, for each of you will be a companion to the other. Now you are two bodies, but there is only one life, one heart, one soul, one love before you. Soon, you will go to your home to enter the days of togetherness. May your days be good and long upon the earth. May you love with everything you are and always be what the other needs."

During the following moment of silence, Abbie felt the last

glittering silver thread of her soul weave itself around Cass's. It was almost complete. They were almost one in every way they were meant to be.

Looking up as Cheveyo began again, Abbie was shocked to see Owen MacAllen, Cass's uncle, standing beside the Chief. Why was he there? Her Mate had said he would be officiating their Dragon Ceremony. But...

"Abigail and Caspian, please remove your blue shawl and blanket."

As soon as they complied, he continued, "As you have discarded the blue of yesteryear, so have you left the past. As you go forward, do so feeling lighter with the love you have found in one another."

"I guess, it's my turn," Owen chuckled. "And I can see you're surprised, Abbie girl. Well, good, 'cause this is my present to you. Tonight, you and Cass will be one in every way intended by the Universe, the Great Creator, God, and The Powers That Be." Pulling a note card from under the tail of his bronze surcoat, he held it up and added, "I even have the Blessing from my boys. No, this doesn't mean we're not gonna have a huge reception at the house after Christmas, cause my wife might kick me in the shins and make me sleep in the barn. It just means Cass here wanted you to have it all on your birthday, and who am I to deny y'all this special gift."

Looking up at her Mate with more happy tears in her eyes, Abbie knew if she spoke aloud she would cry, so instead, she whispered directly into his mind. *"Thank you, Dragon Man. Thank you for everything."*

"Anything for you, my love."

"Okay, so, if y'all are ready, I'm gonna get right to it,"

"Yes, sir," Cass answered for both of them because she could not.

"Long ago, when Knights and Dragons fought side by side for King and Country, it became apparent that Dragon kin was no longer safe from those who would expose, exploit, and destroy them. Seeking to remain hidden but also continue the mission of the Universe to preserve not only their species but humankind, they sought to join with the Knights who had so valiantly fought by their sides for so very many years. Thus, through the Magic of the Original Mage and the Ancient Dragons, and by the will of both Dragon and Knight, the Dragon Shifters were born."

"In the infinite wisdom of the Universe and our Founding Elders, Clans were set up, one for each color of the Dragon Kings whose soul we carry within our own. Each was assigned a region in which to make their home and to protect their families. Over time, some have flourished, some have ceased to exist, and others have been born from the joining of many. As the Leader of the MacAllen Clan of the Bronze Dragons and uncle to the one and only remaining Guardsman and Dragon King of the Dragons of the Clan of the Goddess Maeve, it is an incredible honor to stand here today on the land the Thorntree Cherokee Tribe and the Thorntree Timber Wolves settled and have maintained for centuries. We have always lived our lives on a simple principle–Keep the Great Creator, the Universe, Family, and Love at the center of our world, and we can never fail."

"The Great Creator and the Universe continue to astound one and all as they bless the Dragons with extraordinary Mates for the best among us. Every Dragon who finds the Light of his Soul knows how very sacred she is. It is an honor to witness the power of what the Universe and our Elders put into place at our inception. We acknowledge and bless the Mating of Caspian Thomas MacAllen III to the One the Universe made for him, Abigail Annabella Addams. And now I will read the Blessing from the MacAllen Dragons."

"We, the Dragons of the MacAllen Clan, cousins to Caspian Thomas one and all, wish to witness and offer our Blessing to one born of our blood and the Mate of his heart. May your lives now and forever be a testament to all we hold dear...Love, Honor, and Loyalty. As you are one, let your combined strength see you through many years, and the children of your children's children smile upon you."

Smiling with a twinkle in his eyes, Owen added, "And I am supposed to add, you need to start making babies. The twins need playmates."

Almost fainting, Abbie's mouth started before her brain engaged and she barked with laughter, "As if!"

Bursting with laughter beside her, Cass teased, "Doesn't mean we can't practice...a lot."

"How about we get y'all Mated first?" Owen chuckled. Then, schooling his features, he continued. "The Blue Crystalline Dragons of the Clan of the Goddess Maeve were born from the vastness of the sky and flight. They represent still waters and clouds that carry the Hope for the future. Blue Dragons, especially those blessed by Maeve, are highly protective creatures and extremely Magical. They possess a charitable nature and are larger and stronger than any of the other light-colored Dragons. Blue Crystal Dragons embody the transformative powers of both Dragons and Crystals. They symbolize the journey of personal growth and healing, encouraging individuals to embrace change and release old patterns. Their impenetrable scales protect them in battle, and their ability to take the form of the Warrior Dragon makes them nearly unbeatable. Truth and honor lie at the heart of a Dragon King of the Clan of the

Goddess Maeve and will always be the guiding light in his effort to be whatever his Mate needs. To Mate a Dragon of the Clan of the Goddess Maeve is to accept all that they are and honor the power shared between Mates."

"As the one True and Natural Nûñnë'hï Warrior and part of the Thorntree Cherokee Tribe, do you, Abigail, take this man and his Dragon as not only your Mate but that of your Timber Wolf, Faoiltiama, and the Spirit of the Nûñnë'hï?" Owen asked with authority and reverence in his tone.

"With all that I was, all that I am, all I will ever be, and all that we are together, I accept Caspian and Blár into my heart and my soul. I will share everything that I am with both of these spectacular males every day of our lives together, both here and in the Heavens."

Turning to Cass, Owen asked, "As a Dragon of the Clan of the Goddess Maeve and my nephew, do you, Caspian, take this woman, her Timber Wolf Spirit, and the Spirit of the Nûñnë'hï as not only your Mate but that of your Dragon King?"

"For every day, rain or shine, fire or snow, light or dark, with all that I am or all that I will ever be, I pledge to love, honor, and cherish Abigail, her Timber Wolf Spirit, Faye and her Nûñnë'hï Spirit with all that I am. They will always come first, be the center of my focus, and the love of my heart."

"Now would usually be the time of the Marking, but y'all have a few more things to do, and I am gonna skedaddle. Love one another with everything you got, and everything else will fall in line," Owen beamed. "Barbara and I are never farther away than a shout. We love you both so very much."

Just like that he was gone, and Cheveyo began, "As you can see over to the side, there are two fires burning and the larger pit in the center is still. The two on either side are smaller. They symbolize your life before meeting your Mate. The one in the center is the largest and represents your life as one."

"Go now, Abbie to the right and Caspian to the left. Take the torch, light it in your fire, then together, ignite the larger pit."

Doing as they were told, the crackle of the fire was almost instantaneous, the flames a gorgeous kaleidoscope of yellow, orange, and red-tipped in blue. Reaching for Cass's outstretched hand, Abbie looked into the blaze as Cheveyo continued, "As you look into the sacred flames of your love and your life together, know that your Ancestors are looking upon you with pride. Your union is blessed by them, the Great Creator, and the Universe. Let us pray."

"Above you are the stars. Below you are the stones. As time does pass, remember that like a star, so should your love be constant. Like a stone, your love should be firm. Always be there for one another and be close, but not too close. You must be understanding and grow individually as you grow together. Have patience with the other. Storms will come, but they will go quickly. Be free to give affection and warmth. Make love often and be sensuous to one another. Have no fear and let not the ways of words of the unenlightened give you unease. The Great Creator is with you, now and always. You are Loved. You are Blessed. You are the Everlasting Hope, and together, there is nothing you cannot accomplish."

"Now, I am supposed to tell you that it is time for the Marking. I understand that Caspian has a surprise for Abigail. So, here is where I leave you. Now that I love you both and wish nothing but happiness to you for all the years to come."

Turning toward her Mate, Abbie looked up into his

gorgeous blue eyes and immediately chuckled, "What are you up to, Mr. MacAllen?"

Wrapping his arm around her waist, Cass laid a little kiss on the tip of her nose and winked. "Oh, you just wait and see, Mrs. MacAllen." Lifting her into his embrace, he whispered, "Hold on, my love. We're goin' home."

Chapter Eight

Racing to Abbie's house at the far corner of the Res with his Mate in his arms, all he could think about was being alone with the love of his life. They'd talked about the house his Aunt and Uncle wanted to build for the couple at the Ranch and decided hers was fine for a while–at least until they started a family.

Through the back sliding glass door, down the hall, and he was finally alone with Abbie. There hadn't been a time since he first laid eyes on her in the middle of that grotesque bubble of Black Sorcery that he hadn't wanted to have her all to himself.

Letting her body slide down his, he held her tight, loving the feel of their bodies together. Running his fingers through her silken curls, he loosened her braid until the long, red tresses fell across his hands. The seductive smile curving her tempting lips was everything and only encouraged him to rub and knead down her neck and onto her shoulders.

Pushing the lace off her shoulder, he kissed across her

shoulder to her neck. Paying special attention to the spot he knew would soon wear his Mating mark, he waited until his Mate was breathless before he whispered, *"Tha mo chridhe taobh a-staigh thu a-nis agus gu bràth,"* into her mind.

Allowing the canines of his Dragon king to extend and pierce her delicate skin, he held Abbie up when her knees threatened to buckle. Inhaling deeply, he reveled when, at the same moment, the identical spot on *his* neck stung. Saying the words that had been written on his heart from the moment of his birth, Cass felt the missing piece of his soul click into place. *"Bho a-nis gu deireadh an ama bheir mi gràdh dhut le mo chridhe uile."*

It felt as if his heart had grown wings when Abbie repeated the words in English, her voice breathy and heavy with adoration. "From now until the end of time, I will love you with all my heart, Cass."

Pulling his teeth from her skin, Cass reached around her back as he continued to kiss and taste her neck and shoulders. Needing to feel her body pressed to his, he made quick work of the fifty or so tiny pearl button-snappy things lining her spine.

Capturing her lips as he pushed the soft fabric off her shoulders and down her arms, he smiled into their kiss as her gown floated to the ground. Sliding his hands up her ribs, tracing the band of her bra, his nimble fingers unclasped the hooks, swiftly removing the troublesome garment and throwing it behind him.

Breaking their kiss, loving that Abbie moaned at the loss before opening her lust-soaked eyes and giving him a lazy smile, he chuckled when she asked, "Am I marked as yours, Dragon Man?"

"Yes, ma'am." He looked at the magnificent glowing glyph, the three overlapping arcs–the Triqueta with the wings of his Dragon King on either side decorating the lovely column of her neck. "You are mine now and forever, *Mo chridhe*."

"Good," she sighed. "I do love it when we get it right. It makes everything so much better."

Abbie's mind was only one of the million things he already loved about her. She was not only intelligent, but quick-witted with an amazing heart and body with all the curves in just the right place. She was strong and loving and just everything he'd ever wanted in a Mate, a true partner, and so very much more.

Lifting her into his arms, he kissed her until she was breathless, loving the feel of her body in his arms. Reaching for the last scrap of material covering her body, her silky white panties, Cass rubbed the soft fabric, massaging her heated flesh as Blár growled with satisfaction, pushing him to finish claiming their Mate.

Sassy as ever, just the way he loved her, Abbie put her hand on her hip and with the other hand, extended her index finger, outlined his frame in the air between them, and teased, "Now, it's your turn, Mr. MacAllen."

Standing completely still as she sighed and made a show of rolling her eyes and tsking, he breathed a sigh of relief when she closed the distance between them. He didn't dare move when his amazing Mate slipped her hands underneath the soft cotton of the black turtleneck he wore under his surcoat. Lifting both garments over his head and dropping them to the floor, she ran her hands over his shoulders and across his chest.

Currents of pure white-hot electricity raced through his veins. It filled every fiber of his being and set both man and Dragon alight with the need to be one with their Mate. Slowly shaking her head, Abbie whispered, "Slow down,

Dragon man." Then she ran the tips of her fingers along each ridge of his six-pack before laying her hand on the waistband of his pants.

Unbuttoning the brass button, she demurely looked up at him through her thick, dark lashes before winking. "Do you know how *very* much I love you, and want you, Caspian Thomas MacAllen?"

As if her words had somehow released her succulent scent into the room, Cass inhaled deeply, wishing he could roll in the aroma of the desert, the flowers, McKitterick Creek–of home. Not only was it intoxicating, but it was the perfect complement to his Mate, the woman he loved with everything in him. Shivering at the sensation as the backs of her fingers moved closer to his erection as she pushed his zipper down, Cass held his breath in an effort to not pick Abbie up and ravish her right where they stood.

There was no hiding anything from one another. She wore his mark, and he hers. He'd heard her thoughts and knew that she wanted to take the lead, so no matter how hard it was for him, he would give her what she wanted – always and forever.

Sliding his pants over his hips, her hand bumped his throbbing erection, thrusting Cass over the edge of reason straight into the fiery passion of their combined desire. Unable to hold back, all the resolutions he'd just made fading in the fire of his need, he slid his hands under her arms and held her to his chest.

Using the speed given to him by the Universe, Cass spun around and, within a single heartbeat, had Abbie on her back in the middle of her bed–*their bed*. One more quick move and her legs were over his shoulders, and her center was right in front of his face. Smiling as he rubbed his nose against the wet silk of her panties, he inhaled his Mate's intoxicating scent, sure he would lose his mind if he didn't make love to her right then and right now.

Slipping his fingers under the silk at her hip, he tore the offending material from her body and threw it over his head, growling as the scent of warm, sexy Abigail filled his senses even stronger than just moments before. No longer able to stand the torture of not being joined with her in every way possible, the tip of his tongue slowly licked up the glistening seam of her pussy.

Groaning low in his throat, his Dragon roaring in his head as Abbie's taste burst upon his tongue, Cass knew he'd found Heaven. Placing his hands under the wonderfully round globes of her behind, he lifted her pussy closer to his face, feasting for the first time. It was as of he'd been in the Desert hungering and searching for her–*only her*–for his entire life. Driving his tongue into her excited body as far as he could go, licking every inch of his Mate, he curled the end of his tongue to tease the sensitive bundle of nerves at the top of her channel.

Abbie's hands dove into his hair, fisting the strands and pulling with such force Cass was sure he'd be bald as she moaned his name over and over. Smiling against her silken skin, loving the way she reacted to his touch, he used the flat of his tongue to lick her outer lips from bottom to top, teasing her aroused clit on every pass.

Tightening her legs around his head, her heels digging into his back, Abbie's screams of surrender rattled the windows as he sucked her swollen nub between his lips. Flicking it up and down with his tongue, teasing and taunting, his heart filled to nearly bursting as Abbie shouted her release to the Heavens above.

Lapping at her essence as it flowed from her body, Cass nuzzled and nipped her puffy lips until she released his hair, and her breathing slowed to nearly normal. Slowly sliding her legs from his shoulders, massaging the tired muscles of her thighs, he looked up at Abbie, his body shaking with the love he felt for this very special woman. There had never been a more glorious sight than his very own True and Natural Nûññë'hï Warrior, the one the Universe had made for him, completely satisfied, looking like a Queen laid out before him.

Kissing her hip, then her belly button, where he paid extra attention with the tip of his tongue until Abbie giggled under her breath. Then, he nipped his way up her stomach, kissing the sweet spot between her breasts, loving the feel of her heart beating in sync with his. Palming both her breasts, he gently kneaded, the already raised peaks growing harder against his palms. Kissing up her neck, he smiled against her heated skin as she let her head fall to the side, allowing him all the access he wanted.

True to all he knew of her, his sassy, fiery Mate grabbed his head, pulled his lips to hers and kissed him with the same wild abandon she did everything. Opening immediately, Cass made it clear with his actions that she owned him completely...body, heart, and soul. Just as passionate in bed as she was about everything else, her love fueled him, nourished his soul and made his heart sing–Abbie was absolute perfection.

With her hands in his hair and her tongue sliding in and out of his mouth, dancing alongside his, Cass held back his climax by the thinnest of unraveling threads. Losing the battle, he shifted his hips and thrust his cock into the haven of his Abbie. Pushing until he could go no farther, Abbie pulled her lips from his and screamed, "Cass! Yes! Oh, my Goddess, yes! I love you!"

Wanting to go slow the first time in his Mate's body, he

was unable to keep control as the feel of her muscles contracted around him. Massaging, tempting, teasing, she made it absolutely impossible for him to hold still. Pulling out until only the tip of his rock-hard cock rested within her body, his control shattering with every heartbeat, Cass growled through gritted teeth, "*Look at me, Mo ghràdh*. See the man who loves you more than life itself. You are my everything, Abigail Annabella MacAllen–absolutely the best part of who I am."

Her eyes snapped to his, and the love he saw overflowing from Abbie's heart and soul was nothing short of humbling. Thrusting into her and then pulling right back out, he started a rhythm that she met stroke for stroke with an explosive passion that fed his own. Together in all things, always, that was the gift he'd been given from the Great Creator and the Universe.

Staring into one another's eyes, their hearts beating as one, everything Abbie was reached for everything Cass was a split-second before their passion exploded, rocking both of them to the very bottom of their souls. Still hard and needing his Mate again, he pushed her knees toward her chest, lifted her ass, and went deeper, filling his true love completely.

Rolling his hips, the head of his cock caressed the sensitive bundle of nerves that made the walls of her vagina close tighter and tighter around him. Wanting to shout to the Heavens when her eyes rolled back in her head from the pleasure only he could give her, Cass's chest puffed with pride as Abbie struggled to catch her breath.

Reaching between their bodies, his fingers had barely closed around her clit when her orgasm propelled them both over the edge of ecstasy. Her mouth opened in a silent scream, and her bright eyes held the miraculous promise of all the love in her heart. What was he to do but follow her into the blissful cloud of adoration only they, as one, could create? There was no doubt, and would never be, that Cass would follow Abbie absolutely anywhere, even to the ends of the Earth.

Hours later, they lay together, completely satiated, her head on his chest, their legs intertwined, and their bodies cooling from several incredible hours of lovemaking. Smiling like a giddy little kid from the love he shared with his Mate, Cass reached down and retrieved his pants.

Pulling a small light blue velvet box into the light, he turned to Abbie and laid it in her open hand. Looking up with a shocked look in her eyes, she asked, "What's this? We said we were doing presents after Christmas 'cause we were a little busy."

"No, to be exact, I said you could wait until after Christmas. I was careful not to include myself in that statement, so you couldn't beat me up when I gave you this." His eyes shifted to the box for a half-second, then returned to hers. "Besides, it's not just Christmas, it's your birthday. Open the box, my love."

Opening the lid, Abbie gasped as the ring his momma left to him centuries ago shined in the light of moon streaming through the window. "This is stunning." Her words were little more than the tiniest puff of air. "This is gorgeous." She looked up at him, her eyes glistening with unshed tears. "But it's too much...too beautiful. It was your momma's, wasn't it?"

"Yes, ma'am, it was Mom's, and she left explicit instructions that I was to give it to my Mate." Kissing the tip of her nose, he leaned back and took the ring from the box.

Sliding it onto her finger, he explained, "This is one of

the very rare light blue diamonds in the world. My dad had this ring made the very day he met my mom."

"It is gorgeous. I just..."

Laying his index finger to her lips, cutting off her next rebuttal, Cass looked her right in the eye and adamantly asked, "I'm only doin' what my momma told me to do, so don't sass me."

Raising a single eyebrow but quickly losing her stern façade, Abbie laughed out loud as she wrapped her arms around his neck and purred, "Thank you, Cass. Thank you so very much for everything."

Pretending to tip the imaginary hat on his head and putting even more southern in his voice than was already there, he winked. "My pleasure, Ma'am. I aim to please." Laying his lips to hers, he added telepathically, "And plan to please you every day of our lives together, Mrs. MacAllen, every single day."

"Hot damn, Dragon Man. Merry Christmas, my love, and here's to a very happy new year."

Until we meet again...
May the joy and love of the holidays be with you every day in every way the whole year through.

Hope is the Belief that Anything is Possible

COMING 2025

Waking Her Dragon: Sydney and Garrett's Story

Her Dragon to Save: Return to the Clan, Book 1

Hel Hath No Fury: The Immortals, Book 1

I'm not much of a planner. I write as the character
DEMAND their story be told.
However, in the case of these three books, the characters
have been yelling for a long time! LOL
So, I'm gonna listen and get these out to you ASAP!
Until then...
Take care.
Read lots.
And...
ALWAYS Dare to Dream!
XOXO, Julia

WANT SOME MORE CHRISTMAS DRAGONS?

Check out:

Christmas Magic: Holidays With the Dragons Guard
This box set includes:
Her Dragon's No Angel
Guarding Her Dragon
Tangled In Tinsel
Dragon Got Run Over By A Reindeer
GET YOUR COPY at JuliaMillsAuthor.com!

Holidays with the Dragons
This box set includes:
Dreamin' Of A White Dragon
Dragon, It's Cold Outside
Chestnuts Roasting Over Dragon Fire
A Little Elfin' Around
Whisking Her Dragon Away
GET YOUR COPY at JuliaMillsAuthor.com!

THE STORY THAT STARTED THE WHOLE DRAGON GUARD SERIES

And my life as the Sassy Southern Storyteller -
HER DRAGON TO SLAY!
GET YOUR FREE COPY at
JuliaMillsAuthor.com!

"**D**ammit, Grace, pick up the phone," she growled through gritted teeth at the third voicemail she'd had to listen to in the last five minutes.

"Everything okay, Kyndel?' Barney, the *nice* guy in her office, asked.

"Yeah, everything's fine. Just trying to find Grace."

"Oh! Anything I can help with?"

Kyndel thought about telling him her troubles, but Barney had been spending an excessive amount of time in her office lately. At first, she'd thought he was just being nice, but then he joined her hiking group, and just yesterday he showed up with her favorite no whip, nonfat, iced white chocolate mocha from the *frou-frou* coffee shop on the corner. It had been then Kyndel realized she was Barney's newest crush. It had been a long time between boyfriends and Barney was nice, but...um...*no*. As flattered as she was, there was no way she had an office romance.

'Don't shit where you eat' was one of the pieces of sage advice Granny had given her just after graduation. Not that it ever truly made sense to Kyndel, but she got the gist of it... keep your personal life *out* of the office.

She saw the puppy dog look on Barney's face and hated to crush his spirit, but Kyndel decided a brisk walk home would be better than leading the poor fellow on, in *any* way.

"No, but thank you so much." Then, to make sure he got the hint and skedaddled, she added, "Have a nice a weekend," before turning her chair and dialing Grace's office for the third time.

Voicemail *again*. Time to pack up and get the heck outta dodge before someone found something else for her to do. Bag on shoulder, scowl on face, and more than a little disgusted, Kyndel headed out of the office.

*Never loan Grace the car... Never loan Grace the car...*was the mantra playing on a loop in Kyndel's mind. She was madder than a wet hen and getting hotter by the minute. It was *no fun* to walk home after ten hours of work. *No fun* to be abandoned and forgotten by the best friend she'd loaned her car to. *No fun* to make the five-block journey past the park...in the dark.

At twenty-six, she rarely admitted her fear of the dark and held her aunts responsible for the phobia. Had they not made her watch 'The Brain Eaters' when she was only six years old, Kyndel was positive everything would've been just fine. It wasn't that she believed aliens would set loose a horde of parasites to eat every human brain on the planet; she had a *little* more sense than that. It was the feeling of being watched...like someone was hiding in the shadows, just waiting for an opportunity to scare the living daylights out of her. At the mere thought of her' phantom stalker', the hair stood up at the nape of her neck, and she walked a bit faster.

A sudden *thud,* and what sounded like footsteps pounding on the hard ground, had her stopping in her tracks. "What the...?" She gasped, opening her eyes wide, hoping it would help her see through the shadows.

Several tense seconds later—that felt like damn near forever—and Kyndel moved again. This time, her eyes slid side-to-side like the stupid black and white cat clock her granny used to have in the kitchen.

The farther she got from where she'd heard the 'thump,' the easier it was to convince herself it had just been kids sneaking into the park after hours. Manlove Park was a popular make-out spot for teenagers. There might've even been a time after moving to the city when Kyndel herself had been convinced to take a walk on the wild side, but that was a story for another day.

Shoot, now I wouldn't know the wild side if I tripped and fell in it.

It had been almost a year since she'd dated the muscle-headed jock from the gym. Three long, tortuous dates and all because he had an incredible body. Of course, dating the douche bag had come at a price. She'd spent the entire time listening to him drone on about his body parts...*and not the good ones*...and *only* when he wasn't checking out every other woman in the joint.

It wasn't that he'd hurt her feelings. Kyndel knew who she was and had never been under the misconception she would be Miss America. She had a few extra pounds, and her curves had curves, but she was cute and had a brain, something not everyone could claim. What had pissed her off the most about dating Vinnie was, she'd wasted three whole evenings of her life that she could never get back. The one compliment the jerk had given her had been about her skin; he thought it was beautiful. Her granny always called her complexion peaches and cream and said her freckles added character.

Yeah, cause I need more of that.

She sighed as she thought about how much of her youth she'd wasted hating those tiny brown spots, until the day she realized they weren't going anywhere. It was time to buck up and learn to love them or stop looking in the mirror. From that day forward, she stopped using makeup to cover them and embraced her 'freckled-self.' She also learned to accept her curves. *If ya don't like 'em, don't look at 'em* was her motto. For the most part, she ate right and worked out at least three times a week. But dammit if she didn't love her Ben and Jerry's Cherry Garcia and someone would lose a hand if they tried to take it from her.

A loud *'thud'* echoed between the buildings. Kyndel stumbled to a stop. She looked and listened. The longer she thought about what she'd heard, the easier it was for her to convince herself someone had yelled for help. So, for the second time in about as many minutes, she searched the inky shadows for signs of life. Her anxiety level quadrupled the longer she stood still. She wanted to scream when only the sound of leaves rustling across the sidewalk and the occasional car passing by reached her ears.

Disgusted, she grumbled aloud, "You've gone bonkers, Kyn." The sound of her own voice somehow calmed her rankled nerves, and she added, "Get to stepping, girlie."

The clicking of her heels bounced off the brick wall of

the library as she hurried past. Resuming her original mantra, she added *Must kill Grace* at the end for good measure.

"I swear when I get my hands on..."

Her words were cut short as the unmistakable sound of a man groaning came from the shadows.

A chill skittered down her spine.

Goosebumps covered her arms.

She counted to three, unable to move...simply listening...praying it was only her imagination. One deep breath later, she slid her right foot forward, prepared to make a beeline for home at a high rate of speed.

The groan came again. Closer than before. More desperate...almost pleading.

The need to help the injured grew within her. Turning towards the darkness, Kyndel searched for the source of the noise.

Shaking so much her teeth chattered, she looked for any sign of the man she *knew* needed her help.

"It's time to make a decision, Kyndel. Fight or flight. What's it gonna be? God knows, standing like a bump on a log isn't solving a *damn* thing."

Flight won. She turned, almost running, her satchel clutched tightly to her side like a lifeline.

"Keep your head up and eyes front. Home's only a few blocks away," she reassured herself, with the promise of snatching her best friend bald for the stupid mess she was in.

Feeling guilty and worried for Grace, her heart at war with her brain, Kyndel thought aloud, "Hope everything's okay..."

Grace had always been a little scatter-brained, but she'd never just *forgotten* Kyndel before. It bothered her that there'd been no answer at Grace's office or on her cellphone when Kyndel had tried to track her down before leaving the office. She'd even taken a chance and tried her own home because Grace had a key, but only got voicemail there, too. It was a war between anger and worry that accompanied most of her thoughts about her friend lately.

The running joke was that Grace spent most of her time hooking up with eligible bachelors she met at work. The good Lord *knew* her bestie was gorgeous; five foot nine, long raven hair, blue eyes, and a curvy body without an extra ounce of fat. To top it off, she was a first-year lawyer, with a promising career. Grace had it all...brains and beauty, the total package.

Giggling nervously, she gave herself a mental swat to the back of the head. She didn't want anything bad to happen to Grace, just a bump or bruise, even a hangnail would explain being left. If she really had just forgotten, Kyndel was going to be *pissed* and more than a little hurt.

The shadows seemed to be closing in. Fear pushed Kyndel until she was almost jogging in her sensible work heels. Looking over her shoulder, the toe of her shoe caught an uneven piece of concrete, and from one heartbeat to the next, she was falling forward. Arms flailing, mouth stretched wide in a wordless scream, the sidewalk racing toward her face, everything around her seemed to happen in slow motion. All she could think was *that's gonna leave a mark*.

Bracing for impact, she squeezed her eyes tight and prayed...then nothing happened. Opening one eye, then the other, Kyndel found herself hanging above the sidewalk, looking at a pair of the biggest feet she had ever seen—and they were sexy.

Sexy feet? I really am losing it. Wait! Why the hell am I above the concrete?

Warmth radiated from the perfectly muscled arm wrapped around her midsection. Goosebumps emanated from the extra-large hand holding firmly to her blouse, just a little too close to her breast.

She wiggled to change position, the cushion of her well-rounded ass finding the ridges of an incredibly hard set of abs. She trembled. Her heart raced. Just the thought of the man that could hold her upright made up for all her previous mishaps.

Within just a few seconds, Kyndel's world turned on its axis. The scenery blurred as she was effortlessly spun around and immediately found herself sitting atop the body of her rescuer, looking at faded denim covering extremely muscular thighs. Laughing aloud, she asked herself, *wonder what part I'll see next?*

The same muscled arm that had saved her face from inevitable demise now kept her upright. She did a one-eighty, draped her legs over his thighs, with her knees barely touching the sidewalk, and got her first look at the top half of her rescuer. All she could do was gape. He was absolutely the most handsome man she'd ever seen, with features that looked like they'd been carved by expert hands.

Even with his eyes closed, he gave off the distinctive air of authority. The dim light highlighted his high cheekbones and aristocratic nose, adding to the power she felt radiating from his every pore. His perfectly formed lips made visions of passionate kisses and hot, sweaty nights dance through her brain. It didn't help that all he had on was a pair of well-worn blue jeans.

She imagined that denim riding low on his tapered hips when he stood, highlighting the incredibly sexy dimples that sat on the front of his hips. She absolutely knew without looking they were there, and that simple bit of knowledge made her temperature rise another degree, despite the cool breeze.

At the touch of her fingertips against the cool skin of his neck, an electric current arced between them. Flashes of light burst before her eyes. She blinked to clear her vision, then felt for his pulse, strong and steady against her digit. Heat rose from his skin, making her worry he might have a fever. Her eyes wandered down his well-toned body. She scoffed, unsuccessfully trying to convince herself she was only checking for further injury.

Who the hell do you think you're fooling?

She continued her perusal, taking note of his massive shoulders and a chest that could've been sculpted from granite. The light smattering of hair that glistened in the shards of light from the streetlamps emphasized his nipples, which were pebbled from the cool breeze. Her mouth watered, and her pulse raced.

What the hell is it about this guy? Is he doused in pheromones? Or am I in heat?

Her eyes landed on the best set of abs she'd ever seen. Unable, or maybe it was unwilling, to stop her hand, she traced the defined lines of his eight-pack, mesmerized by the feel of his skin beneath her fingers. The electricity continued to flow between them. The sound of a horn in the distance pulled her from her musing and brought her current situation into the glaring light of reality. The sexy man that had kept her from breaking her face on the concrete was out cold, and she was paying him back by sitting on his lap and copping a feel.

She scrambled to her feet, surprised her rescuer hadn't moved an inch during her less than graceful attempt to remove her butt from his lap. But there he lay, unmoving, except for the rise and fall of his chest. The longer he remained unconscious, the more panicked she became.

Looking up and down the street and cursing Grace for the hundredth time, Kyndel wished for her car. First Aid class had taught her *never* to move an injured person unless you knew what was wrong. Not that she could pick him up and carry him, anyway. The dude was *HUGE*. At least six-foot-three or four, and his muscles had muscles. She prayed he hadn't hit his head on the sidewalk. A concussion could be really bad if not treated.

"You're worried about a concussion now?" She scolded herself. "You've been drooling over the guy while his head is lying on the cold, hard sidewalk. Brilliant, Kyn, just brilliant." Reaching for her satchel, she grabbed her old sorority sweatshirt from inside, wadded it up, and knelt forward to lift his head.

Her fingers tangled in his soft, brown hair. The scattered shards of light made it look like melted chocolate flowing over her skin.

Would it shine in the sun or maybe have highlights? Some lighter brown mixed with red, even a few blond streaks woven throughout?

The silky softness of his tresses turned to something wet and sticky.

Blood!

Kyndel gulped. Panic seized the breath in her lungs as the true severity of the situation smacked her in the face. She fought to keep her calm. Now, there was absolutely no denying he needed medical attention. Reaching into her bag and cursing herself for not thinking of it sooner, she dug around for her cellphone.

Coming up empty-handed, she instantly remembered plugging it into her car charger the night before, not giving it the slightest thought until that moment. Cursing and threatening death to anyone in the immediate vicinity, she sat back on her heels and thought.

All I know to do is run down the street for help.

Looking at the fallen man, then in the direction of the Mini Mart, she reasoned he'd probably be okay. She'd be gone five minutes...*tops*. Run in, use the phone, run back. It all seemed very logical, but fear something would happen to him in her absence kept her in place.

This guy was important to her. That alone had all her red flags flying and bells and whistles screaming in her brain. She tried to push her feelings aside and look at the situation with logic, but that was like holding back a freight train with her pinky finger...*not gonna happen*. Besides, her granny would most definitely haunt her and probably kick her butt if she turned her back on someone who needed help.

"No one's gonna mess with this behemoth, even if he *is* unconscious," she reassured herself. "He probably doesn't have a wallet to steal anyway."

Should she dig in his pockets to try to find one? Some kind of ID?

Nah.

She wasn't keen on trying to explain her hand in his pants if he woke up. Her cheeks warmed at the thought of touching him again.

"What are you doing out at night in just a pair of jeans and bare feet, anyway?" she asked the unconscious man. "Guess it doesn't matter. You need help, whether you're dressed properly or not."

Hooking her satchel over her shoulder, Kyndel stood and took one last look at her 'patient.' Before she had barely moved an inch, a large, warm hand latched onto her bare ankle.

"What the hell?" she screamed, trying to pull her leg free while looking down to see what new fresh hell had befallen her.

READ THE WHOLE STORY!
IT'S FREE at JuliaMillsAuthor.com!

ABOUT JULIA

From the bottom of my big, ole Southern Heart,
THANK YOU! THANK YOU! THANK YOU!
Without YOU, the Reader, I would be lost!
And these crazy Dragons, well, they just wouldn't know
what to do with themselves.

Somewhere along this journey, I wrote these words:
I was born with a love for all people everywhere, a vivid
imagination, and the gift of gab! So, even though it took
forty-six years, I finally found what I was meant to be–A
STORYTELLER!
It not only allows the characters in my head to tell their
fantastic tales, but I get to meet the most AMAZING people.
(YES! THAT'S YOU! The wonderful person who's reading
these words right this minute!)

Suffice it to say, you have made every word I write possible
and for that~I will never have the proper words to THANK
YOU!!!

OH! One more thing! In case you don't know, I LOVE STALKERS! The easiest place to find all my links is **at JuliaMillsAuthor.com.**

Take Care!

Read Lots!

And ALWAYS Dare to Dream!

XOXO, Julia

ALSO BY JULIA

Dragon Guard Order
1.Her Dragon to Slay
2.Her Dragon's Fire
3.Haunted by Her Dragon
4.For the Love of Her Dragon
5.Saved by Her Dragon
Her Love, Her Dragon, A Dragon Guard Prequel
6.Only for Her Dragon
7.Fighting for Her Dragon
8.Her Dragon's Heart
9.Her Dragon's Soul

10.The Fate of Her Dragon

11.Her Dragon's No Angel

12.Her Dragon, His Demon

13, Resurrecting Her Dragon

14. The Scars of Her Dragon

15. Her Mad Dragon

16. Tears for Her Dragon

17, Guarding Her Dragon

18. Sassing Her Dragon

19. Kiss of Her Dragon

20. Claws, Class, and a Whole Lotta Sass

21. Dragon with the Girl Tattoo

22. Dragon Down

23. Twinkle, Twinkle, Sassy Little Star

24. Dragon Got Your Tongue

25. Fury

26, Dragon in the Mist

27. Dragon Got Run Over by A Reindeer

28. Tangled in Tinsel

29. Cupcake Kisses & Dragon Dreams

30. Her Dragon's Treasure

31. Aww Snap, Dragon

32. Imagine Dragon

33. Save a Horse, Ride a Dragon

34. Burn Dragon Burn

35. She Thinks My Dragon's Sexy

36. Dreamin' of a White Dragon

37. Dragon Her Home

38. Stone Cold Protector

39. Dragon's Lore

40. King Outta Water

41. Dragon, It's Cold Outside

42. Dragon, Be Mine

∼

Dragon Guard Collections

∼

Dragon Intelligence Agency

∼

Dragon Guard Berserkers

~

Ladies of the Sky
Sadie's Shadow

~

Kings of the Blood
Viktor
Roman
Achilles
Kings of the Blood, Books 1 - 3

~

Dragons of Fate
Chestnuts Roasting Over Dragon Fire
Unwrapping Her Dragon
She Needs A Little Dragon
Falling Off Her Dragon
The Dragon of Valentine's Past
Dragons of Fate Collection, Books 1 - 4

~

Dragon of Destiny
Dragon Him Out To Sea

~

Dragon Guard Holiday Love Stories
It's The Great Dragon, Molly Brown
A Little Elfin' Around

Heart On For Dragon
Dragons Fall Hard
Dragon Guard Holiday Love Stories, Books 1 -3

∼

Not Quite Holiday Love Stories
Kissing Cupid
Kissing Claws

∼

Maidens of Mayhem
That Hound Don't Hunt
That Pig Gonna Fly
That Mule's Got A Kick
That Rex Gotta Roar
That Shark is Red Hot
That Dino's Hanging Ten
That Dragon Gonna Blow

∼

Not Quite Love Stories
Vidalia
Phoebe
Zoey
Jax
Heidi
Lola
Sammie Jo
Harmony
Daphne

≈

Magic & Mayhem Collections
The Not Quite Collection Volume 1
The Not Quite Collection Volume 2
Maidens of Mayhem Collection Volume 3
Maidens of Mayhem Collection Volume 4

≈

Southern Fried Sass
Later Gator
Nosey Rosie
Lazy Daisy
Jamie's Got A Wand
Southern Fried Sass: Volume 1

≈

Up Shift Creek
Tree Frog and Her Honey Badger
Doc and Her Dragon
Dusty and Her Dino

≈

Daughters of Poseidon
Out of the Ashes
Scorched Embers

≈

Lords of Hell

Hades Halo

∽

A Vampire's Thirst: Alaric

∽

Condemned: A Vampire Blood Courtesan Romance
Caught: A Vampire Blood Courtesan Romance

∽

Marrok: Hunger For His Mate

∽

Coloring Books
Bitch Please! I Color Dragons
Witch Please! I Color Dragons
Dragons of Legend Coloring Book

∽

Planners
The Dragon Never Sleeps
No Rest for The Dragon

∽

Reading Journals
On the Wings of Words

JOIN THE CLAN!

Wanna Keep Up With All My Crazy? Wanna have fun? Win some cool prizes? Get exclusive excerpts to upcoming books?Sign up for my newsletter RIGHT HERE!
Be the FIRST to see new covers, sneak peeks, and best of all, ADVANCED COPIES OF ALL MY BOOKS!!!
Join the group! Julia's Mills' Fan Club on Facebook!
I absolutely LOVE stalkers!
You can find the links to follow me everywhere at JuliaMillsAuthor.com!

Fate Will Not Be Denied

Julia Mills

·SASSY·SOUTHERN·STORYTELLER·

Fate Will Not Be Denied

JuliaMillsAuthor.com

9 798230 993834